T0065248

IN THE LIFE OF
NZURI

Nzuri

iUniverse®

IN THE LIFE OF NZURI

iUniverse books may be ordered through booksellers or by contacting:

iUniverse
1663 Liberty Drive
Bloomington, IN 47403
www.iuniverse.com
844-349-9409

ISBN: 978-1-6632-1484-3 (sc)
ISBN: 978-1-6632-1485-0 (e)

Library of Congress Control Number: 2020924895

Print information available on the last page.

iUniverse rev. date: 12/14/2020

This is a story about a free woman, who once was lost
but now is found; who once was blind, but now sees.
Her captor had her totally convinced that if she did not do
what he told her that she would lose her life
like those two fine officers that lost their lives
in the line of duty.

DEDICATION

I give honor and glory to God Almighty!

*To Every Victim of Domestic Violence and Sexual Abuse
Around The World...You Matter!*

<u>Psalm 139: 13–16 (NKJV)</u>

*"For you formed my inward parts; You
covered me in my mother's womb.
I will praise you, for I am fearfully and wonderfully made;
Marvelous are your works, and that my soul knows very well.
My frame was not hidden from you, when I was made in secret
And skillfully wrought in the lowest parts of the earth.
Your eyes saw my substance being yet unformed.
And in your book, they all were written
— the days fashioned for me,
when as yet, there were none of them."*

If You Only Believe

"Jesus said to him,
If you can believe, all things are possible to him who believes.
Immediately the father of the child
cried out and said with tears,
Lord, I believe; help my unbelief!"
Mark 9:23–24 (NKJV)

"My little children, let us not love in word or in tongue, but in deed and in truth."

I John 3:18 (NKJV)

TABLE OF CONTENTS

CHAPTER 1

GROWING UP DOWN SOUTH

MY NAME IS Nzuri and this story is about the early years of my life.

I was born in Philadelphia, Pennsylvania on Thanksgiving Day 1976. Philly is where my parents met. I grew up, down in, South Carolina. I was very young when my family moved to South Carolina. My father's hometown was in, Puerto Rico. My mom's hometown was in, South Carolina. I remember having so many adventures with my siblings and cousins in the South. The Spring and Autumn were my favorite seasons. You could smell the fresh flowers growing and see how beautiful the trees and grass were. I used to love the sweet and sour weeds, the black berries, the honeysuckles, the figs, the plums, and so much more that grew around us that was edible. I used to love it when my grandmother washed clothes.

When the water poured down to the ground from the washer machine, it made streams of water sufficient enough for mud pies. The wet mud felt so good in my hands and on my feet. We would play for hours outside. By the time our moms called us inside, we had to go straight to the tub to wash. In my mind, it was all worth it. My parents moved from the city because it was hard for my dad to find work. My mom said that her plan was not to move permanently back home, but my father seemed to enjoy living down South. Dad said that he was tired of the traffic in the city, not to mention the cold weather. They were supposed to eventually move to Florida, but it never happened.

My parents were hard workers and no matter what, they did not give up on their dreams of overcoming poverty. They worked together to make things better for our family and their hard work paid off in time. We started out living behind my grandparents on their property, but eventually my parents bought property of their own in a different area of South Carolina. This happened around the time my mom was pregnant with my youngest sister, Dawn. My oldest sister Wanda and I shared a room together; and at age 4, I was still a bed wetter. I remember how concerned my mother was for me. She finally came out and asked me if anyone had ever inappropriately touched me and I told her "No." No matter how hard I tried, I still had difficulty controlling my bladder. My mother was frustrated, and I was confused. If we traveled long distance, I could not drink a lot of liquid because I would have to suddenly use the bathroom. However, I later learned that an older step–cousin had molested my oldest sister and me when he babysat us. At the time, I was under age 1 and my sister Wanda was 2 years old. Wanda remembered this man fondling us after sending my brother and cousin (which was his younger brother) outside. My parents were not aware that the incident had taken place until my sister Wanda finally said something about it as a young adult. I know they would have done something about the situation if they had known.

My mom and I did not have the best relationship growing up and there was much to be desired. I was baptized at 5 years old and I always felt close to God. Around the age of 8, I became an overweight child and struggled with insecurities like bed wetting. My mother does not believe that she treated me any different than my siblings, but she did whether she would ever admit to it or not. I know I was not a perfect child. However, I feel that my mother did not know how to help me with my obesity and insecurities. She did try even though some of her tactics were objectionable. I remember my mom making me put my hands on the Bible to make me tell the truth about taking food and other things. I hated that! I knew if I told her the truth, she would beat me, so I lied. I remember feeling so awful about lying. My dad did not treat me that way, but through the years, he stopped disputing my mom about the unpleasant things she said and did to me. I was withdrawn as a child and my mom would ask me if I was depressed. I was, but I did not know how to express myself to my mom. I felt like no one around me understood. I was screaming inside for help, for someone to save me from what I was going through. I remember contemplating suicide at one time when I was a teenager. I was going to take a bunch of

Tylenols, but I could only swallow about three. I remembered fearing God for trying to commit suicide.

I am so glad I knew Jesus at a young age and wanted to live for the Lord.

I remembered the Scripture that references serving God in your youth when you could do more for Him and not to wait until you are old and limited.

I decided that I wanted to represent for other young ladies by living my life as a positive role model. So, I decided that I was going to do the right thing so that other young girls would not think they had to follow along with the so-called "majority" who wanted to have babies at a young age or just wanted to party. However, I went overboard with my methods. I tried to make people feel guilty about not serving the Lord like I did. I went around witnessing to people in the wrong way instead of living my life so that others in darkness could see God's marvelous light through me and give their lives to Christ Jesus.

I tried to live my life to please my parents. I grew up in a family that was not rich but had accomplished much from hard work. My family was very concerned about their children doing well in life, including living for Christ, graduating from high school, and going to college or into the military. These are the things we looked forward to accomplishing. We were in church almost every time the church doors were open, and we participated in all the activities: youth choir, adult choir, usher board, open service, etc. My aunt Carrie was my role model when I was growing up. She was our Sunday school teacher when we were young. My aunt was one of the first female ministers in our area. She is a strong woman of faith, and I admire and respect her. She was always nice and helpful to everyone.

I tried to make good grades. I stayed out of trouble in school. I did what my parents asked me to do around the house, but it never seemed to be enough for my mom. When I was transferred to a new elementary school, there was a female classmate who used to bully me because she was jealous that I was new and many of the boys liked me. This girl was aggressive, and I told my teacher what was going on. I also mentioned it to my mom, so she was aware of the situation. One day I had finally had enough of this girl bothering me.

While we were yelling at each other on the playground, someone pushed her against me, and we started fighting. There was a crowd of kids that surrounded and compelled us to fight. My teacher did not punish me because she knew that the girl was bullying me. My mom had to come to a meeting at school to be debriefed about what happened. When my mom got home from the meeting, she spanked me because I engaged in the fight. During this same week, the girl's mom came to the school while we were in line waiting for my teacher to walk into our classroom. The mom waved her hands in my face and threatened me while her daughter laughed. I was scared and I told my teacher, but the incident was never addressed. I was upset with my mom because she punished me instead of supporting me against this bully! Thereafter, the young lady and I became friends, but it was hard for me to trust anyone. What happened to me as a child affected my decisions as a young adult. My mom told me as a young adult, that I was a smart child. I know that God knows what every child of His needs to get them where they need to be. My trials and tribulations have made me a strong woman.

If I had not gone through what I have been through, then I would not have known what is inside of me. How would I have known what I can endure? There are not many people who are willing to admit the type of trauma that I experienced and seek professional help to heal. It is sad because an entire family can go through life confused and divided. It takes consistent prayer and love from everyone involved to conquer such unhealthy behavior. The enemy wants families to believe that there is no hope for their situations to improve, but that is a lie from the pit of Hell. Love never fails and love conquers all things. Things can change if we are willing to do what is necessary to realize the desired change. After all, it has taken many years, but they are changing for me and my mom. I love her so much!

To this day, our relationship has changed with a better understanding of each other and I am going to continue to pray for more changes.

"Indeed, we count them blessed who endure. You have heard of the perseverance of Job and seen the end intended by The Lord that The Lord is very compassionate and merciful."
James 5:11 (NKJV)

"Hatred stirs up strife, but love covers all sins."
Proverbs 10:12 (NKJV)

"Blows that hurt cleanse away evil, as do stripes the inner depths of the heart."
Proverbs 20:30 (NKJV)

CHAPTER 2

FIRST CRUSH

A T AGE 13, I was a very independent young lady. I started out babysitting for one of my teachers in the 9th grade. During the summertime, I started working with my Cousin Ella, who had a cleaning business. We began to bond and establish a spiritual relationship. She is a Prophetess of God and she told me God wanted her to "take me under her wings." I became my Cousin Ella's assistant on the job.

She encouraged me and made me feel I was important. I am so thankful for her.

After my summer job with Cousin Ella ended, I worked in a seasonal position at a shoe store with my oldest sister Wanda for the Easter holiday.

After the holiday was over, Wanda was hired as part–time

staff, because they only had one position open. This did not stop me from wanting to work. You develop a sense of responsibility and healthy pride when you can work and make your own money versus having to depend on money from your parents. I wanted to help my parents by helping myself. I urged my mom to help me find a job. I got hired at Burger King but was not satisfied with that job. So, before Wanda went to college, I went back to the shoe store to ask for her position and got it. By doing this, I learned that having connections can be a rewarding advantage.

Now, I was a dedicated employee, an 11th grader, and 17 years old.

Being employed gave me space from my mom and it gave me the opportunity to meet interesting people. Additionally, not being sedentary at home gave me the means to lose weight. I was feeling good about myself and this is when I met my first boyfriend, James. He was a year younger than me, cute, and funny. I was always self–conscious about my weight. I was intentional about not dating guys at my high school because I did not want people talking about my personal business. My brother, Felix told me earlier in life to be careful of guys because they liked to abuse full–figured girls and talk bad about them. He may not have believed that I was listening, but I was. My numerous male cousins openly talked about how they used girls and made fun of them all the time. There were other guys that came around and wanted to date me, but there was something about James that made him stand out. James was a foster child who lived with foster brothers. I did not know why he was in foster care or what had happened to his family. As I got to know James, I found out that he was friends with some of my close friends who dated some of his foster brothers. Knowing this made me more comfortable with James because my friends said they were a fun group of young men. He would come by my job daily after school. He would keep me company sometimes when I had to work shifts alone. I made sure to check with my manager, Donna, who had become a good friend of mine. Donna was cool with it and did not mind. Besides, her boyfriend, Hank, would do the same for her when she had to work alone.

James came into my life at a time when I was tired of being the good girl.

I was ready to have fun and take chances. I was that child that listened to my elders and was smart enough to be in honor classes, but I was not motivated. I wish someone had helped to motivate me in being more diligent with my education.

I made decent grades but only did enough to get by in school. I felt like everyone thought I had it together when I really did not. Now, I encourage adults to reach out to young people who seem to have it together. They need attention sometimes just like the young people who are not doing so well. Good children need guidance and encouragement, too. I would have progressed further in life if I had been more focused then. Receiving information from your friends is not a good thing either. How can anyone my age provide advice if they have not yet experienced certain things in life to help them mature? This experience is called "wisdom." I heard so many cousins and friends talk about their relationships with their boyfriends and girlfriends. In my mind, I desired to have a nice boyfriend who cared about me, did not get into trouble, and was not involved in criminal activities. I also desired to be with someone who did not drink, smoke, or use drugs, just like me.

James was an athlete and took care of his body, at least he was always bragging about this.

Peer pressure was tough, especially when you saw your family and friends around you having a good time. It makes you feel like you are alone when everyone else around you is enjoying their life. My family kept us sheltered so I was not prepared for someone like James. He gave me so much attention and I was not used to this at home or anywhere for that matter. I believed that he cared for me, and he had this tough guy attitude that I liked. He was consistent with his words and gave me gifts all the time. He did not have a driver's license, but if he told me he would meet me somewhere, he would be there. He became my first crush. James would always talk about his foster dad and his foster dad's son, with whom he was close.

I could tell by the way he spoke of his foster dad that he must have been a very caring man. They were Sabbath worshippers and were regularly in church like my family. At the beginning of our relationship, his foster dad had died. James was so sad over this happening. When he called and told me about it, one of my best friends and I rushed over to his house. I received my first speeding ticket when driving to get there. I was sad for him. I was looking forward to meeting his foster dad but did not get the opportunity. I met his foster mom, and I could tell she did not care too much for me. I had a car and would sneak around with James.

I am sure how James and I hung out had something to do with how she felt about me.

Eventually, James started using my car while I was working. This went on for a while. He would sneak me through his window, and then we started getting caught by his foster mom and their maid on numerous occasions. At times, James would be on punishment and would sneak out the house to be with me. He was my first love and I made him wait a long time before being intimate. He appeared not to have a problem with my decision and that made me respect and love him even more. I knew I could never tell my mom or dad what was going on. James would make out with me to the point I thought I would lose inhibitions, but he would never penetrate me. I did not know much about sex, but I learned how to masturbate at a young age. I had the aching feeling at a young age, so I would masturbate when I got home from making out with James. When I decided to start having sex with him, we would park somewhere secluded and make out. James was not very good at foreplay, but he was a good kisser. He would let me straddle him in the car and let me have my way with him as much as I wanted. Sometimes, he would be asleep while I straddled him. I would lose count of how many times I had an orgasm. Every opportunity that I could have sex with James, I did. I was scared to go to his house, but we would have sex there too.

I cannot ever remember my parents giving me permission to date, and I was a senior in high school when I met James. The only thing my parents would tell us was, "Just don't have sex" and that was all we needed to know. I knew about condoms from my friends, and I eventually went to the local clinic to get on birth control because I was old enough to sign for it without my mother's consent.

Most of my social life growing up consisted with hanging around close family and friends and going to church functions. One of my cousins graduated with a newborn baby, and so many other teenagers younger than her were having babies at my school. My dad seemed like he got stricter with rules because of that.

My plans for myself, at a young age, were to be a role model and show other young girls that they did not have to become a statistic and become a teenage mom. I had set out to enjoy my life, work hard, and have children later when I was able to afford them. This was the plan. I graduated from high school and I was very happy that I had not become pregnant. I had accomplished that much so far.

I continued working at the shoe store and then enrolled in nail technician training, which was two nights a week. I also secured another part–time job as a waitress at Denny's. Shortly thereafter, I received the Assistant Store Manager position at the shoe store. I traded my owned car for a newer sports car.

My dad talked my mom into co–signing for me to receive a lower interest rate.

I was so surprised that my mom did it, but she fussed about it. I was on my way to accomplishing my goals but also nearing the end of my relationship with James but did not know it.

James and I had been dating nearly two years when he started getting into trouble — at least that was when I started realizing things were going on.

James started asking to borrow my car overnight so he could work. I never knew what kind of job. I was just happy that he was working. I was scared because I would have to sneak out of my window at night just to take him home and bring back my car. It got to the point to where he started sneaking through my window because it was so late. I got into a big argument with my mother once because we were caught. I left the house with James and went to one of my good friend's home. This is when things between James and me started to spiral out of control.

I had found a place to rent and had such a miserable time with James taking my car and leaving me alone. When he would return, it would be late, and we would argue about his whereabouts. This is when I started feeling betrayed by James, because I was in this situation for defending him to my mother.

I lost my job at the shoe store because my boss told me that my cash drawer was short. She knew that I was very careful with my drawer and I never had any prior problems with my job performance. I was fired by the District Manager and he said that they were going to investigate. I just knew that I deposited my night register bag like clockwork. There were more checks than cash. I was so confused as to who would set me up like this. I never once had any thoughts of ever taking something from anywhere or anyone that was not mine. I remember telling myself that things could not get any worse than this.

Shortly afterwards, James took me to meet his biological father. I do not know what happened between them, but I knew James was upset when we left his father's house. When I asked him what was wrong, he would not say anything.

He told me that his biological mother was also living, but I never got to meet her.

I do not know if James knew where she was.

James started getting into serious trouble and ended up in jail a couple of times. I bailed him out once or twice. Who wants to see their "boo" locked up if they can help them out? His foster mother became angry with me for what I did, but I still did not know what was happening with James' situation. I just knew that I loved him and wanted to be with him. There was one time that I found out that James got arrested for assaulting a man and this was a felony charge. During this time, James and I did not talk on a regular basis. I had left my parent's home and moved in with one of my cousins because my mom and I were still not getting along. I got into big trouble because of James and another inmate, escaping from the detention center. Who escapes from the county lock up? He set up me and another girl that he was "dating." He asked me to go to the projects adjacent to the detention center and wait. When I arrived, this other girl arrived shortly afterwards. I felt jealous seeing her there. I never thought I had a reason to not trust James. The thought never entered my mind that James could be a cheater.

When we recognized one another from visiting at the detention center, I lowered my car window and asked if I could talk with her. I thought she was the person he wanted me to see. Her name was Heather. I was confused about why James wanted me to go to the projects. After talking to Heather, it appeared that neither one of us knew why we were there. I thought that he was going to call me at someone's house that he knew out there to talk to him on their telephone.

We had to pay so much for the phone call, and I thought he asked someone he knew to allow us to talk on their phone. Instead, he tried to use me and Heather to help him and another inmate escape from the detention center. I was so terrified with what was happening and afraid for my life! I could not believe that James was escaping from the detention center. The fence had barbed wires and was very high! It felt like a dream when I saw them running towards my car. Later, when I was questioned by the police, I was afraid. I did not tell them immediately what I knew, but eventually I answered whatever questions they asked.

My parents came to my aid and picked me up from jail after I was released on my own recognizance. I did not cry at first while I was in jail, but I cried profusely during the car ride home. I was rebellious toward my parents regarding James, but they never turned their backs on me. The detective said that he did not have a problem with releasing me because I helped with the investigation. James had tried to use me and Heather. To add insult to injury, Heather was pregnant by him. What a betrayal! Poor naïve me!

When I crossed paths with Heather after this incident, she informed me that she had suffered a miscarriage. I did not have any emotions for James or Heather. All I was thinking about was restoration from the shame and embarrassment I was feeling, including my name being in the newspapers. I knew that everyone around town was talking about me. However, I was helpless in proving my innocence to anyone about what James had planned. How could you use somebody you say you loved?! I felt even worst for the man that James assaulted. I was told that he had broken into the man's home and tried to rob him. James ended up going to prison. My mom told me that I could not help James, even though I tried. I found out later that they became pen pals, but my mom never told me she was writing him.

I found letters that he wrote back to her. I guess she figured that she could help him. I felt sad because I knew James was having a rough time with life and wished I could have helped him. For me, I went to a youth offender's program that gave me the opportunity for a second chance. I had to pay a fine and do community service. When my community service hours were completed, my records were expunged. By God's grace, I got a second chance!

Through this drama, I learned not to say that things cannot get worse because they did for me. My world was turned upside down, mainly because of my affiliation with someone I loved who got caught up in criminal activity. If I was guilty of anything, it was guilt by association. Why is it so hard for young people to recognize emotionally unhealthy people when they meet them? For me, I think that I was just so happy to have someone to care about me. My life had this void that

I could not fill. I was looking for love and acceptance in the wrong places.

As innocent as it may seem, I was naïve about the things that happened and did not have a clue about how bad the situation was with James. My life could have been ruined by association with James.

To all young people, I say: Please do not be deceived

by association with family members or friends that are not moving in a positive direction. Run fast from troublemakers, and do not allow yourself to be consumed by doing wrong. If they love or care about you like they say they do, they will never put your freedom or life in harm's way. You have nothing to prove, except that you should never accept this kind of behavior from anyone. Your life is valuable and has purpose!

The enemy hit me hard, but I fought for my life. I believed that God had a purpose for my life and that is why these incidents happened. I was hurt but learned that trials and tribulations arose in my life to make me strong. I am a living witness that you can rise above any adversity or anyone who tries to drag you down into their mess.

"My son, if sinners entice you, Do not consent.
If they say, "Come with us, Let us lie in wait to shed blood;
Let us lurk secretly for the innocent without cause;
Let us swallow them alive like Sheol,
And whole, like those who go down to the Pit;
We shall find all kinds of precious possessions,
We shall fill our houses with spoil;
Cast in your lot among us,
Let us all have one purse"
My son, do not walk in the way with them,
Keep your foot from their path;
For their feet run to evil,
And they make haste to shed blood.
Surely in vain the net is spread in the sight of any bird;
But they lie in wait for their own blood,
They lurk secretly for their own lives.
So are the ways of everyone who is greedy for gain;
It takes away the life of its owners."

Proverbs 1:10-19 (NKJV)

In the beginning of time when Adam and Eve sinned against
God, women were not only cursed to experience the pains of
giving birth to children, but Genesis 3:16 also says that, "your
desire shall be for your husband, and he shall rule over you."
In the early days of The Bible, a man was a woman's
husband once he had sexual intercourse with her.
We, as women, must be very careful of who we give ourselves
to because sexual intimacy is meant to be a sacred blessing not
a curse, but a woman's desire towards that man is a curse.

CHAPTER 3

EMOTIONALLY BLINDED

I DECIDED TO MOVE out of my parents' house to move in with a friend I met as a nail salon customer at my new job. She was looking for a roommate and she lived a short distance from my job. This was after the mess I went through with James. I was over him and had decided to move on with my life. I stopped visiting him after going to jail behind his mess. My roommate was also trying to get over the problems she was having with her boyfriend. I was still ride sharing in South Carolina with some of my lady peers from the hair salon. These ladies treated me with so much love and respect and cared enough to help me. Now that I lived closer, I could walk to work. I was almost 20 years old at the time. I was slightly nervous being out on my own.

One late night, I decided to do my laundry. The laundry room was open all night. I had my clothes sorted out in the washers and headed back to my apartment. When I went back to check on my laundry, I saw this strange man standing in the dark. I was afraid and went back to the apartment to ask my roommate to come with me. She and I walked outside together; and sure enough, the guy was still there. She had this bright idea of us introducing ourselves to this stranger. I went along with it. To my surprise, the guy said "hello" to us, but he did not stop staring at me. I was so used to other females getting all the attention from guys. We talked for a while and I noticed that my roommate kindly excused herself. I and this guy walked back to the laundry room and talked there all night into the morning.

We both shared about ourselves, including him just being released from prison in Georgia. He would not go into details about how long he had been there because he said he was falsely accused of the crime. I did not pry because I figured he had his reasons for feeling that way. He helped me take my laundry back to my apartment door. He was such a gentleman. I was blushing because he kept staring into my eyes. I never had anyone stare at me like that. Tyree said he was 35 years old. I remembered Cousin Ella prophesying to me that I would meet a man who would be in his thirties. She also mentioned that some older men looked good for their age. I thought, "I don't want to be in a relationship with an older man, but I liked him." My friends and I used to say that older men are bossy and think they know everything. We did not have any interest in dating an older man. However, Tyree looked good for his age and he talked about more than the average guys I knew. By the end of our conversation that night, I had learned that two of my regular manicure customers were related to him — his mother and youngest sister.

They were very nice to me and faithful clients. I really liked the idea that I knew this man's mother. He asked me if he could call me. He was honest with me thus far, so I did not have any problem with seeing him again. Besides, he came from good people and I thought that he was a good person, too. I also believed that everyone deserved a second chance in life. For all I knew, he may have been innocent. I intentionally did not give him my phone number that night because

I wanted to see if he would seek me out again.

One day, Tyree surprised me and showed up to my apartment uninvited.

He came with a handful of old books. My roommate was working on the day that he came by. We talked at length. He started asking me questions about Black History and I was embarrassed about the things I did not know. He educated me on how ancient black people were kings and queens and how successful black people have been from the beginning of civilization in Africa. He also said that the Africans that were gathered for the slave trades were amongst the smartest and lived civilized lives. I was so engaged in what he was saying. I have a love and appreciation for my people and always wanted to know more about our cultural history. When I was a teenager, my ex–brother in–law was the first person who shared with me about Black History and how the meaning "Pro Black" was about cultural pride not what others wrongly thought. Tyree shared about his desire to start a church and how important it was to be active in our community.

He also shared with me how he had a special name set aside for his wife and how he was waiting for the right woman to marry. The name he had was "Nzuri."

I thought the name was different and beautiful. He said the name meant "someone who is beautiful," — not just outward beauty, but also inner beauty. At first,

I thought: What?! What woman would change their birth name just because her husband wanted her to? Tyree explained to me later that he had many Swahili and Hebrew names that he would later use for the people in his congregation.

Getting to know Tyree for the first year was very interesting. I remember talking to one of my cousins the next day and telling her that I believed I met my husband. It was a feeling that came over me. He shared so much information that was beneficial to me. He was a male companion with whom I had fun.

Tyree said if I could just trust him, he had a plan that would help us to "come up" in life. I still had trust issues and I needed time to think about what he said.

I always had led myself and still had a distance to go. After thoughtful thinking, I decided I would take a chance with Tyree. I figured if it did not work out, I could just move on. I was young and I needed my life to start coming together.

The first thing Tyree asked me to do was to move back into my parents' house to save money. I did not want to do that, but humbled myself to ask my mom and dad to move back in. To my surprise, they said yes but under certain circumstances.

I still had an 11:00 p.m. curfew and I now had to pay rent. The next task was reinsuring my vehicle. Tyree had this plan thought through. I was surprised and happy. Finally, someone was helping me to get somewhere in life! I did everything the way he told me to and saw results. My mom was the first person to whom I introduced Tyree. She perccived and told me he was too fast for me. I did not get along with my mother, so I received what she said as hurtful. However, in retrospect, she was right. I wish I would have listened to her then, because her insight could have saved me from a series of problems. Tyree shared his insight on my work environment, and I started becoming more successful at work. I started making more money and he wanted me to give him a portion of the money to save. I was nervous about it, but everything the man had been telling me to do was working out so far, so I did it. He had found a job and explained the importance of saving money and spending wisely. He eventually opened a bank account in his and his younger sister's names. They were the only two that could access the account. I felt that he should have had my name on the account too, but he always had a way of justifying what he was doing. For example, when I found out he was dating other women, he said he was using them to give him money for us. He started living with a woman, too.

I thought this was crazy! I only heard of this behavior on television. He told me that he wanted to move out of his mother's home to gain more freedom. We had been dating approximately six months and had become intimate in our relationship. To be honest, I do not remember the sex being anything more than an every "blue moon" for Tyree to cum. He never tried to make love with me or wait for me to have an orgasm. I confronted him about the womanizing, and I told him I did not want to be hurt or share him. He asked me to meet him in person to talk about this and I did.

He explained to me how important I was to him and how he wanted me to be his #1 lady. He said those other women did not mean anything to him and everything he was doing was for us. I cried and wanted to walk away from him, but this man had already helped me to accomplish so many things that I thought was impossible to do. He was teaching me new & interesting things and I wanted more of what I was learning. "What should I do?!," I thought. Tyree could be so convincing. He held me, kissed me, and told me everything would be alright. He explained how all of this was to help us. It took me a while to process through my feelings, but I decided to continue with our relationship. From the beginning of our relationship, I felt that this was the man prophesied to be the one for me. I believed that this man was everything I wanted in a mate, but I was inexperienced. I assumed this man would change his ways for me if we were married. So, I suppressed my feelings about his improprieties. I was so wrong in thinking this way.

The lady who helped to start my nail technician career was opening an all–nail salon, which would be the first African–American owned nail salon in South Carolina.

We had become popular at the hair salon, but we had potential customers that did not want to come to us because we worked with beauticians. Some of our new customers were also beauticians that came and supported us after we moved out of the hair salon. Many of their clients came to support us too. I decided to make the move with her because she had promised to reduce my booth rent and I was learning from her — nail techniques, information on different products, and much more. We were very professional with our business and we did not get into each other's personal lives.

I really enjoyed working with her. She was older than me and was like a big sister. When she opened her salon, our business quadrupled. We eventually had two other women working with us. Disappointingly, she did not keep her word to reduce my rent, but my status was much better working with her. She would help my business to progressively grow as an independent contractor.

Tyree also encouraged the move. However, it was concerning to learn that he started hanging out with people that were rumored to be drug dealers. He had about three different jobs at the time. One of them was at a night club owned by the husband of my nail salon owner colleague. Tyree was also friends with her brother. One day, Tyree found a good deal on a sporty motorcycle.

He used some of the money in our bank account for a down payment and financed the rest. Tyree started calling me Nzuri. He would take me out and treat me like a lady. We would go out to dinner and hang out all the time. Tyree would even take me out on walks in the rain under an umbrella. We would hold hands and embrace all the time. He was such a gentleman to me. He also made sure I was home before my curfew so I would not get in trouble with my mom. Initially, I was scared to ride on the motorcycle. Eventually, Tyree helped me become comfortable with riding on the back like a pro. What surprised me was that this man never made me feel uncomfortable about my weight! He had been encouraging me to lose weight and explained how beautiful I was. Tyree reminded me what the name "Nzuri" meant.

He said I would be one of the finest women around if I lost weight. I told him how much I wanted to, but I did not believe I could do it. I had tried so many times and had failed miserably every time. I told him about my mom's techniques and how she used to embarrass me for being overweight. He said he believed I could and that he would help me. He said he would not force me to do it, but he would wait on me to make the decision to receive his help. I did start following Tyree's lead on eating better and exercising. He went out and bought us both bicycles because I told him I loved bicycles. He gave me pointers about exercising and many other tips about health and fitness. When we first started dating, Tyree requested for me not to tell anyone that he was my boyfriend. However, he said it was alright to say that we were dating now.

One day Tyree's youngest brother came to town unexpectantly. He asked me if it was okay for him to smoke a black & mild and drink one bottle of St. Ides with his brother. Tyree's reasoning was he had not seen his brother, who had been in the military, for so long. I told him that was his decision to make. Prior to that day, I had never smelled cigarettes or alcohol on Tyree. He was a big advocate for being healthy. After that day, I never saw him drink, smoke, or even have the aroma of either on him.

One day while I was working, Tyree came to my job with a line of police officers following him. While they were handcuffing him, he told me that he was innocent of the charges. Later, I discovered that Tyree was arrested for a minor marijuana charge. He said that he and some other guy decided to trick an undercover agent into buying a bag of crushed leaves that looked like marijuana. As I recall, he was the only one that got arrested. This was the beginning of things changing. When it was time to go to court for his trial hearing, he wanted me to accompany him. Tyree had been teaching me about being a Hebrew and taught me how Jesus was a Hebrew. I was enjoying what I was learning, and I was also in a world of turmoil behind it. He made it seem like almost everything I had learned in church was not true. I had days when I went to church and was sad for the entire service because I thought my pastor was being hypocritical. Tyree had a way with convincing you through the Bible and other books that he was correct about what he was explaining. He had convinced me why I should not eat pork and purchased a book for me to read about it. He spoke about the importance of wearing my hair natural. It was very rare for a man to wear locks in South Carolina, even more so for a woman. I may have been one out of two that did. I felt like I had something to prove to Tyree. He made this seem like a competition to see who would become his wife and I had convinced myself that I wanted to be the one. I wanted to show Tyree I could meet the challenges he gave me.

Tyree had found a place for us to rent. He had planned to sign the lease the same day his trial was scheduled. He had also surprised me and paid a deposit on buying a male Rottweiler puppy for me. He planned to pick up the puppy a week after we moved into the trailer home. I was excited and afraid because he had been schooling me on what to do if he was "found guilty." Tyree's attorney requested that we come to court dressed up. This meant that he would have to wear a suit and he hated suits. I had to pick him up from one of his girlfriend's houses the morning of the trial. When we arrived in court, his case was soon called. He and his attorney approached the bench. After hearing all the evidence, the judge told Tyree if he could pass a urine test, he would release Tyree. I felt confident that he was going to pass this test because Tyree was not a drug user. When it was time for the test results, his attorney and I sat next to each other and the judge told him that the test was positive for marijuana. The attorney started swearing and asking me if I was smoking with him. I replied, "No!" I did not know what this man was talking about.

The judge sentenced him to one year in prison. Tyree appeared to be disappointed as the court officer handcuffed him. I left the courthouse sad and lonely. I could not believe what was happening. After leaving the courthouse, the attorney approached me for the remainder of his fees. Tyree had mentioned to me before court that if he did not beat the case, do not give the attorney anything. He instructed me to use the money to rent the home. He told me not to tell anyone, especially the landlord, about his prison sentencing. Tyree requested that I inform people, with whom he was working, that he was out of town. He was thorough about his instructions and I followed them exactly. A few days later, Tyree left word with his youngest sister to have me go to his mother's house to talk to him on the phone. He gave me further instructions on what to do, including set-up of a home phone service and to make sure it included receiving calls from the prison. He also said he was tired of babying me and it was time for me to step up and be the woman he knew I could be.

He was talking abrasively to me, but I took it as positive criticism to ensure

I could survive. I would officially be living in an unknown community by myself with no family or friends, nearby. No roommates would be living with me.

He included me losing weight as a part of the terms and conditions to stay in an intimate relationship with him. He said there were other women who would be glad to switch places with me. Once again, I looked at it as though he was doing me a favor by choosing me to be his lady. So, I embraced the challenge. It was a while before I heard anything else from him due to prison processes. I assumed there was no turning back and I wanted to make him proud of me.

My dad helped me move my belongings into the rented mobile home. My mom also came along. She did not have much to say. I was happy to be independent. I lived approximately 10 minutes from my job so that was great, too. Tyree ended up being incarcerated for 13 months because of bad behavior. I wrote him just about every day, along with sending him pictures as he requested. I visited him every weekend and on holidays. I was making good money at work, so I would send him money weekly. He monitored my weight loss progress and gave me pointers on how to reach the goal he had set for me. I was very happy with my progress — so happy that I exercised every day. I was reading my Bible every day and started praying three times a day. Tyree would give me positive feedback on my progress when he saw me on our visits. His feedback made me want to work harder too.

Tyree also started calling me his "Queen". Some of his friends from prison would call me "Queen" too and that became my nickname.

He would share with them my progress and show my pictures. He also wanted me to legally change my name to "Nzuri". I started using the name at work on my business cards, and politely asked people around me to use that name. This was a step closer to legally changing my name permanently, but not yet. When I came home from visiting him, I felt so lonely again. He would call me when he thought I had made it home to check on me. I hardly visited or spoke to many people, because I felt like my life was changing and I did not have much in common with many of them anymore.

My sisters, cousins and I used to sing together in church and at different functions. We sang so well together, and many people enjoyed hearing us.

I believed, that if we had kept singing, we probably could have had a bestselling album. For years, I regretted giving up that joyful activity. Tyree's youngest sister and her boyfriend would visit and keep me company. They helped me around the house because I had to keep the yard maintained. My dad bought me a lawn mower to make the maintenance easier. His mom and stepdad also supported me, and they always treated me kindly. If I needed anything, I would go to them first most of the time. One day, Tyree and I were talking on the phone and he asked me how I felt about polygamous relationships. I told him that the Bible references its existence in history, but it is no longer a legal lifestyle. This was not a topic I wanted to discuss. He never said anymore about it. However, he was adamant about me finding a young lady and befriending her. He told me that I was going to need someone with whom I could be close. I had thought it was strange of him asking me to do that, but that was as far as my thoughts went.

When Tyree finally came out of prison, he was a totally different person.

He was not trying to hide from me who he was anymore. Right before he came home, he told me that he would marry me if I were 150 pounds and had at least $2,000.00 saved in the bank account. I tried my best to live up to the challenge.

He would always try to bring up these other women who wanted him and would take my place if I did not do what he asked me to do. It was like there was always someone else competing for his love and attention. Really?! Nevertheless, I had got myself together and I felt like I had come too far in this relationship to have someone else beat me out. I was competing for this man's love and affection.

He would tell me, "Oh, you are going to be the mother of the church and you are going to be the one representing." Before he got home from prison, he had asked me to purchase a gallon of Hennessey and a gallon of Gin. He said he had been locked up and he wanted to chill out for a while before he started working again.

When he finally got home, it was just before my 22nd birthday.

He asked me about the bank account and asked me to get on the scale. The bank account was a little over $2,000.00 and I was exactly at 150 pounds. Wow! I had lost 135 pounds. He grabbed me and hugged me. We were both smiling from ear to ear. For me, that was a challenge I thought I would have never been able to do and I did it! I really believed that I owed Tyree so much. This man had helped me to improve my life and I was so thankful to him. We had sex but Tyree did not make love with me. I do not remember the sex being memorable. It just took place. He mentioned that he would teach me how to have sex, as though I was an amateur. I thought

I knew what I was doing; but as far as he was concerned, I did not. I just wrote it off in my mind that he was 15 years older and that he had more experience with sex than me. He told me that he was going to marry me and wanted us to legally change our names. I know that people do change their names, but that fact did not stop me from feeling nervous. Tyree had been teaching and guiding me and I did not want to disappoint him. So, one week later, we signed a marriage license and the name change documents on the same day. We had decided we would start trying to have children once I was 23 years old. I told him I wanted to enjoy my new body for a while before having children and begin to enjoy our marriage.

In the middle of our first week back together, Tyree picked me up from work and had cleaned up my car. The trunk was filled with laundry. He wanted to stop by the house first to get some liquor. Tyree wanted me to drink too because he said he was still celebrating his release from prison. I did not want to drink but did not want him to think that I was being a party pooper. While en route to the laundry mat, we got into a terrible car accident. I had just made the last payment on my car and this accident split my car in half with only the front seats still intact. The other driver was a Caucasian pregnant female. She was driving for a pizza delivery company. We were riding into a winding curve when the accident occurred.

I remember Tyree acting crazy at the wheel before the accident happened.

He was saying that his uncle was a race car driver and taught him how to drive.

He started driving faster and I begged him to please slow down. Before I could grab my seat belt to help get a grip, I heard a loud bang, and I was knocked out.

When I awoke, we were left in the front half of the car. All the rest of the car was out of sight. If someone had been in the back seat, they may have not survived. Tyree was arrested for the accident and this was my first incident of witnessing how cops could be corrupt. I thank God for being so kind and gracious to me. I came out of the accident without one scratch on me. On the other hand, Tyree was so messed up. I thought he was dead on the scene. He was not moving or breathing.

Later, he told me that he had seen a bright light. I remember praying so hard that night for God to save him. He was unconscious and his chest bent the steering wheel. At the hospital, while they were wheeling Tyree out to the police car, one of the patrol officers handed me a big paper bag with some money in it and two big, empty cans of beer. I asked, "What is this?" He said it was a bag that belonged to me. I told the officer, "That doesn't belong to me!" The officer walked away and said nothing. They were trying to set–up Tyree for this accident with planted evidence. I knew that we were not drinking out of those beer cans because Tyree had a juice container with the liquor in it. My family was there; and of course, they were not happy about my personal changes and were probably afraid for me too. I was disgusted with this situation. I ended up going home with Tyree's mom, stepdad, and his youngest sister where I would avoid hearing "I told you so."

Tyree got out of jail as soon as we were able to pay his bond. It took him a while to recover, but he did. He was a strong man. A week after the accident, we received our marriage license; and since Tyree's stepfather was a notary, he asked him to sign it for us. There was never a wedding, just the marriage license. We also received our official name change documents. Tyree hired an attorney to defend him in the car accident case. He said there was no way he was going back to prison. The lady involved lost an eye and her baby lived.

I was so thankful! The accident was a sign, but that was not how I viewed it. I pitied this man who just came out of prison not even a week ago. I continued to work in the nail salon with back pain while Tyree recovered at home. I was also working overnight at Walmart as a cashier and decided to resign.

Tyree started hanging out with my neighbors who were Caucasian. I always spoke to them in passing, but never hung out with them. Shortly afterwards, he was encouraging me to hang out with them. We would play video games and they would be smoking marijuana and drinking, except for me. They were cool, but he knew

I was not used to this type of company. He told me if they offered me a bottle of wine cooler, just act like I was drinking it so they would not think I was the "popo." I sure did not want them to think I was a cop, so I did as he asked. Tyree would be smoking marijuana with them. One day I saw a group of people in a bedroom, passing around a tray with white powder. Tyree stepped in the room with them and told me he would be back. I do not know if he indulged or not, but I had my reservations. After a while, we became friends for a long time with these young people. One of the young ladies and I had become very close. She was subdued like I was and did not go for all that foolishness with the wild partying and hard drinking, but she loved to smoke "weed." Tyree was always over to their house and they loved him. He was this older cool black dude, and he could entertain.

He always knew what to do or say to get someone's interest. From that point, it was more about what he could get into for himself than what he could do for the church or teaching me things about the Bible. He started hanging around more young people who were my age or younger than me. He always boasted about what girl wanted to be with him or how good a girl looked, even if she had a boyfriend. He would always brag about how good he looked at his age and how strong he was.

Maybe, because he had been incarcerated for so long, he did not age much.

Tyree finally got a job with the help of one of our Caucasian neighbors.

This gentleman was the only one closer to Tyree's age. We could finally start saving up to move out of our current residence into a better environment.

The first time Tyree laid his hands on me was in 1999. We were "play wrestling" in the house after we had sex; and suddenly, he got his belt and started whipping me. He whipped me so hard and long that it seemed like he was never going to stop! I was pleading and crying for him to stop but he would not stop whipping me! When he finally stopped, he calmly told me that he never wanted me to think in my mind that I was strong enough to defeat him. I was bruised all over with whelps, especially in my hands from trying to protect my naked body.

My hands were so bruised that I thought my pinky fingers were broken. He never apologized! I remembered older women telling me, "If a man hits you once, he will do it again." I was afraid of him, but I did not believe in giving up on marriage.

This man had done so much for me when no one else cared to help. It did not justify him whipping me, but I was willing to persevere. I thought that if I did what he said and did not make him upset, this would not happen again.

A couple of weeks later Tyree told me that we were going to start looking into buying a home and planned to be in one in six months. He mentioned that everyone was going to be jealous of me because I was married to a good–looking man, I did not yet have any children, and I was going to become a young home owner.

Tyree said many older women did not have this status. Tyree would say many of them were sad and lonely, but not me. He said I had much going for me. He was able to find me a home in half the time he had planned. When Tyree was in prison, I paid our bills on time like he told me and both of us had great credit at this point to buy whatever we wanted. He negotiated and was able to get a brand-new, double wide, mobile home with no money down. My dad agreed to give us property he had near my grandparents. We only made a verbal agreement about the property.

My mom asked to see our marriage license. I was like, "Is she kidding me?" She was very skeptical about many things so that did not bother me. I was able to select from three homes that Tyree had chosen. I was so happy and excited! I worked extra hours to come up with the money we needed to set up our home. Tyree told me that he did not want me to see the home until he had completed some landscaping. He got very upset with me and hurt my feelings when I expressed wanting to see it once it was delivered onto the property. Right then, his words came back into my heart. He had once told me, "What seemed to be a curse could be a blessing, and what seemed to be a blessing could be a curse." I felt awful when I heard these words in my spirit and it pricked my heart. It still was not enough to run away from my newfound life, but I know what I heard. My family came out to see the home and they were very happy for us. The home was beautiful, and it came with some new furniture. Now, I had a husband, a home, and vehicles including a motorcycle. All these materialistic things did not mean much to me. I felt blessed, but it did not make me feel that I was better than anyone else. When we moved into our new home, Tyree continued working for about a month or two, then he decided to take off and rest some. He said I should be able to work and make a living for both of us now. Then, about a month later he started working with my father doing drywall. He eventually found an excuse to stop doing that and it just seemed like he did not want to work! I think he was just being lazy! This was surprising to me because there was a time when he worked three jobs at once.

Months passed and Tyree would hang out in the streets with his friends while I was at work. This became the new normal for us. I did not hang out with them and he did not bring them around. He would only invite our former neighbors to visit. One day Tyree came home and told me about this young lady who was homeless and needed a place to stay. I told him no way did I want another female living in my home! He must be crazy! Then, Tyree started emphasizing her being needy and feeding me nonsense about how this girl could contribute to building his church.

He wanted to start his ministry. Tyree was interested in recruiting people that were needy in various ways, neglected, and mostly young. I felt compassion because he said that the young lady was homeless, and I allowed him to bring the young lady to meet me. She was 19 years old. He made it seem like she was being mistreated. She was the first female to come live with us, but she was not the last.

Later, he came to me and asked if he could sleep with this girl so he could gain control over her. What?!?! I could not believe what I was hearing! I told him "No!" He said having sex with women gave him power over them. He wanted me to allow this girl to come into our bedroom and for me to give him permission to be intimate with her and me together. This was one of the many things he tried to make me do. Due to the fear of him, I succumbed to his desires. I was forced by him to unwillingly participate in uncharacteristic behavior. We were all lying in the bed naked and Tyree started to rub on both of us and rolled on a condom. He penetrated me first, pulled out of me, and then started having sex with the young lady. I told him I was leaving! He rolled his eyes and waved his hands for me to leave while he continued to please himself. My moral upbringing was strong, and I did not turn away from what was in my heart no matter what he tried to make me do.

He tried to justify his actions, including incorrectly using the Bible. He said if he was not doing it behind my back and I knew about it, it was not a sin. What a twisted lie! He would tell me, that for a man to have multiple wives, he had to be able to afford them. He did not have any money, if that was the case. By the way, even though this girl knew this was my husband, she still agreed to be intimate with him.

I do not know what else he said to the young lady, but she continued staying with us. I tried to treat her with disdain so she would leave, but Tyree's influence over her was so strong. He was happy that he had someone with whom he could drink and smoke marijuana because he knew I was not interested in that type of socializing.

As time passed, he would hold me down and blow the smoke in my face to make me catch a contact. They thought it was funny! The young lady told Tyree about her younger sister, who was almost seventeen. The sister hung out at this African village in South Carolina, where they practiced polygamous relationships.

She said to him, in my presence, she believed once Tyree met her sister that he was going to "kick her to the curb." The sister was not homeless and lived with their father and stepmom. They also had some brothers who were older and did not play games but that did not stop Tyree. It was a couple of weeks later when the sister came to visit, and she had just turned 17 years old. Tyree was now 38 years old.

This girl became his other woman. He would take her on motorcycle rides, and they would stay out for hours. This girl would wear skimpy clothes and be hanging all over Tyree — hugging and kissing him in my presence. He would make me ride in the back of our vehicle and let her sit in the front seat. Tyree was so into her that he stated to me he could marry her, because he was not married to me under his new name. She knew about me as well, but she acted like she did not care. I am sure that the same way Tyree repeatedly manipulated me, he had done that to her too.

Who knows what he had her believing? These girls did whatever he told them to do. He took us out to one of the baseball games in South Carolina, where there was always a huge crowd. I was so embarrassed. He had two girls walking on each side of him, and I was left to trail behind them. He did not care that he was out in the open around my family and other people I knew.

One day Tyree had to go over to his mom's house and wanted me to drive him there. He threatened me the whole way there concerning these girls. He was mentally abusive but did not hit me since the time he whipped me with the belt. I know that the relationship was really changing between him and me. On our way back home, he told me that he was falling out of love with me and I told him I was falling out of love with him, too. Suddenly, he slapped me so hard in my face that I almost swerved off the road. He told me to pull over! This was off the road where a company sold storage houses and you could not see the road. He yelled at me, "Get out of the car!"

I was so afraid. He had this cold & uncaring look in his

eyes. He demanded for me to come toward him; and when I did, he slapped me repeatedly. He slapped me so hard that I collapsed to the ground and started seeing "dizzying stars." He told me to get up or he was going to kick me. I stumbled getting up. He told me if I did not get it together, he was going to make me suffer then told me to get back in the car.

I just wanted to run away from what I was going through. When we made it back to our house, I went to the bedroom to be alone and cry. He came in the room and started taking his clothes off. He told me to get ready. I told him that I did not want to have sex with him. He did not care because he forced himself on me anyway.

This was not the first or last time this happened. When he was done, he put his clothes back on and left to go back with the girls. He called me out of the room later and told the two sisters how he punished me out on the road. I felt so humiliated.

I remember the former girlfriend he beat up and how he took me to see her.

Tyree was using me as an example to instill fear in these girls. I could see it in their eyes that they were scared.

One week later, my mom and dad came by for a surprise visit. Tyree made me go in the room with him and told the girls to say we were not at home. My parents waited for a while and my mom asked the girls, "Why are you here?" and "Why weren't we home? He waited until they left to come out of the room. Of course, he would talk about my parents after they left. He would say cruel things about them and say they were snooping. After a while, Tyree told the older girl she had to get out. They both were sad, but the younger girl continued staying with us. They had an older sister who was supposed to take the middle sister in. I could not sleep nor eat. One morning, I finally had enough courage to confront him. I got up and knocked on the bedroom door where the two of them were sleeping. I told him that I had to talk to him. He came out of the room with only a towel wrapped around his waist. He said, "What is going on Queen? What is wrong with you?"

I said in a low voice, "Look, I cannot do this. You have to choose — either me or her." I told him if he wanted, he could have his relationship with that girl. I did not care. I told him I was losing my mind and I just did not want to have any parts of what he was doing. He looked at me and I saw that scary look again. He started hitting me and throwing me around! He tossed me up and threw me against the wall and made the wall cave in. The towel fell from his waist, but he continued to beat me up! I wanted to hit him back, but I never hit him back. I was afraid that if I hit him, he would really hurt me. I knew I wanted to live through this. I screamed at the top of my lungs! He beat me bad that day. I was so afraid, and I did not know what to do or where to go. Tyree left the room and said he would be back, and I better not leave. I wanted to leave the house and run away, but I was so afraid that he would come in and catch me. One of my aunts lived next door to us, but I was so afraid that it would be the first place he looked. I knew I did not want to get my aunt involved with what was happening. I saw a hammer in the room. I do not know where the hammer came from, but I hid it under my pillow so I could use it to defend myself. When he came back, he asked me where I put the hammer and he checked under my pillow. I was shocked that he saw the hammer! Tyree held the hammer in his hands while he looked at me with that terrifying look and told me to get in the tub. He started telling me how tired he was of me always complaining and fussing about things he was doing. Tyree told me that he did not want to get blood all over the place so that was why he wanted me in the tub. I begged and pleaded for my life repeatedly to him. I remember that I had cried so much until it was hard for anymore tears to come out of my eyes. I never felt such fear for my life like at that moment. I kept saying, "Please let me go" and "I'm so sorry". He threatened my life again and told me not to come out of the tub as he was leaving the room. He let me know that he was not letting me go and he was going to be with this girl.

After all of this, I had some appointments that day at work and I was still the only one working in this house! We had so many overdue bills to pay and I was pulling the load to keep us afloat. He was still spending money on weed and alcohol. His little mistress smoked marijuana, too. This was something Tyree had to have every day and he did not care what went lacking. I did not want to go to work this day, but he made me. I did not have a vehicle to drive and we only had the truck his stepdad gave him and the motorcycle. He dropped me off and picked me up from work because he rode around all day. He said he and his new wife were heading to Hilton Head to spend the day while I went to work. When Tyree dropped me off to work, he said, "Don't do anything stupid! You ain't shit and your pussy ain't shit! Nobody wants you!" I did not believe him when he tried to degrade me and play mind games with me. Tyree could not stop me from believing that I was a good woman in every way, but I was hurt and sad. I felt like no one understood what I was going through, and I was afraid to tell anyone what was happening.

My life at home was starting to affect my performance on my job. How do you tell someone that your husband is abusing you and is having sex with other women under your roof? I never spoke with my co-workers about it, but I am sure they had an idea about what was happening. I put on a face at work the best I could like nothing was wrong. I knew that my friend that owned the salon knew what type of man Tyree was. He even accused her of wanting to sleep with him. Everybody wanted him was what he always claimed! I opened the salon door, sat, and cried as

I waited for my first customer to come in. When she arrived, I hardly said anything to her at first. I wanted someone to talk to, but I was so afraid. I was the only one at work on that Sunday and I decided to vent with my customer. Tears started to well up in my eyes and told her about the incident that happened that morning.

She was so easy to talk to. She told me about her experience with domestic violence and told me how her life had totally changed. She had married a man that now treated her so well. At first, I could not believe that she had gone through domestic violence because she had looked so peaceful. She said she really loved her new relationship and her husband really loved her. Her testimony gave me so much hope that my life could change for the better, too. I told her that I was afraid to go back home and that I wanted to leave this man. She asked me if I was serious about wanting to leave. I said yes! She took me back home so I could get some clothes and helped me to leave Tyree. I grabbed all the money that we had, including the money that his new girlfriend had given him to help with the bills. She said her daughter was traveling back home to Columbia, South Carolina. At the time, that was what I really wanted. I wanted to start my life all over. I was tired of feeling so depressed and so alone. It was like my eyes were so cloudy and I could not believe I was allowing this to happen to me. I could not believe that this man was controlling my life this way. I spoke with my customer's daughter as well and she asked me the same question, "Are you sure this is what you wanted to do?" I said yes. This lady, along with her children, took me back to her home in Columbia. She did not ask me for anything. She only asked how she could help me. I felt so loved by God.

This man was causing all kind of division between my family and I; and the relationship between my mom and me had gotten worse. This compassionate lady allowed me to sleep in her home and was going to help me find a job. They were some beautiful people. She was also a social worker and probably had interacted with other women like me in situations like this and just wanted to help. I was so grateful to her for helping me.

I was afraid that Tyree would come to look for me. So I cut my locks so that if he did, he would not recognize me. I called and had the electricity disconnected and anything else that was in my name. I said that if he was going to be with other women, they were not going to use anything in my name, including the house, which I was also willing to let go. All that I had been and sacrificed for this man, and he acted like my faithfulness to him meant nothing! I knew that God did not want me to be so unhappy and mistreated. I had decided that being faithful in this relationship was not for him, but for me. I believed in my heart that one day life would be better for me and that I would reap what I had sown. One day I would be with someone who treated me with deserving love and respect.

My plan was to find a salon to work in during the day and to find an overnight job like I did before Tyree came out of prison. After a few days went by, I wanted to know how Tyree and his mistress were getting along. I purchased a calling card and called his mother's house to speak to his sister because I believed that she would know what was going on. She told me that he was there and said that he wanted to talk to me. I hesitated because I was not expecting him to be at their house. I was so nervous, but I had decided to talk to him. To my surprise, he was very humble and was talking so kind to me. He told me he took the young lady back home and that he did not have any electricity or food. I never knew this man could be so sad about me leaving him. It made me feel like I had struck a chord in him and he was finally willing to change. Maybe, there was a chance for our relationship after all. He put his sister on the phone for her to tell me how bad off he was. He started crying on the phone and begged me to please come back to him. I had all kinds of emotions running through me and I knew I still loved this man. I did not marry him to see my marriage end without enduring the rocky start. I did not forget that he hit me, but I did believe that if he really meant what he was saying, I was willing to give him another chance. Besides, I was prophesied to about a man like him, so I went back! I waited about two weeks, but

I did go back. What I did know is that I was taking a chance because I knew I would not be able to come back to the lady's home once I went back to Tyree. She and I sat down and talked about it before I left Columbia. Maybe, he was ready to do right by me or maybe he wanted to do worse things to me because he was upset with me. I did not know.

I returned to the nail salon where I worked, and the owner had changed the locks. She said I could not come back because Tyree had harassed her and the customers looking for me. Tyree did not know that this lady and I kept in touch with each other from the time I left. He started accusing me of losing my job and allowing my personal problems to get in the way of my job. Was he kidding me?!

It was because of him that all these things were happening! This was the start of the nightmare happening all over again. He was using this situation to make me think I was irresponsible. I was so deeply hurt because I soon discovered that the former nail salon owner colleague, to whom I dedicated so much time and energy, was scandalizing my name and telling my customers and everyone else about what happened between me and Tyree. I could understand her not wanting me to return because of what Tyree did, but why punish me for that. I never did anything disrespectful towards her. She and I had been together so long. I felt so betrayed by her! So, I had to turn one of my rooms in the house into a nail salon. Some of my customers came, but my clientele mostly continued patronizing the salon. My nail technician career was never the same from that time forward.

Tyree went through a period of wanting to be a drug dealer and sold the motorcycle so he could get a pound of weed and some cash. He was smoking more than anything and since I did not want him to sell drugs, I told him it was better that he used it for himself so he would not have to go around looking for marijuana to smoke every day. Tyree also went through a period of breaking into people's homes with one of his friends. I knew he did not go out and buy the possessions that were brought into the house; and I was not there to know exactly what he was doing. For someone who did not want to go back to prison, he sure was not acting accordingly. The friend eventually got locked up and did not "snitch" on Tyree. He did not seem to have any remorse about this guy sacrificing his freedom for him.

At this point, along with doing nails at home, I went back to full–time employment at Walmart. I started not caring to save anything anymore. I silently took Tyree's criticism because I was afraid that he would try to make a point by hurting me again. He would speak negatively about his own mother and loved calling her a "bitch." Tyree started back inviting people over to smoke weed and drink while he told his stories about being in the prison system, the Bible, and shared knowledge about the lives of black people in America. I felt like I was there to watch over these young people, like some type of motherly figure, protecting them from Tyree. Tyree always had some type of A, B, C and even D plan up his sleeves.

This time his backup plan was a young lady named Kim. He said he had known this young lady for some time, and he was waiting for her to turn 17 years old.

He sent me and his younger sister to go to the house of the young lady's mother to pick her up. He said this girl's family was mistreating her. He gave me the sad story about how she needed somewhere to live and could be helpful to me. He did not bother to tell the young lady that he was married until she came to the house.

Kim was different from the rest. This young lady was very humble and hardly came out of her room. He would say that she was just happy to be out of her mom's home and just wanted to sleep because she was tired. He really did not pay much attention to Kim, which surprised me.

Tyree continued working on the non–profit application for his "church" and started having bible study more often with the young people who hung out with him at our home. The young people would invite their friends who would come faithfully to hear Tyree teach and smoke weed. There were those moments when he had so much to say about the history of the Bible and I was all ears. The information was refreshing to me, and I wanted to learn more about the Ancient Hebrews and our God. Everyone would share how they felt about all the new knowledge Tyree was teaching us about the Bible and books that were not included in the King James Version. He would say he did not like that King James was a child molester and how Christians used the Bible that King James wrote. Tyree managed to get his non–profit application approved, and I remember thinking that this man is very smart. If he would use his ability for good, he could do so much for God's people.

He named the church, "The People of God," because he said an angel spoke that name to him when he was incarcerated in Georgia. He appointed people to different roles. My role was to be the "Church Mother," as he had told me from the beginning of our relationship. Tyree had given some members Hebrew and Swahili names. None of the other members ever legally changed their names to my knowledge.

He would boast about how he was able to obtain the non–profit approval for the church and how so many church folks were too dumb to get the process done.

Sometimes, Tyree would humiliate me in front of the young people in public and blame me for the unpaid bills. Sadly, he was not trying to work!

He tried to stir up ongoing confusion between me and my family to distance our relationship more than anything. I know how many of my family members felt towards him and he knew that too. They did not like what he was doing to me and all the life changes they observed were unsettling and unacceptable to them.

My grandmother was bold enough to say to him: "You're sleeping with those young girls." He tried to deny it, but he knew she was right. At times, he would introduce them as my cousins to strangers or family members that he respected. I felt so emotionally torn between my family and him. I felt like I was being used in the middle of confusion and discord. The frequent mistreatment towards me by Tyree was sometimes so bad that I felt, if I did not end my relationship with this man, he is going to kill me. I left Tyree so many other times after the first time.

However, I repeatedly came back for various reasons. I would always justify to myself that he would change and that was the right thing to do.

Eventually, I stopped running away after I was almost in a terrible car accident while traveling to South Carolina. I had to swerve from hitting a tire on the freeway. God was with me, and it was a miracle that I did not lose control of the car. God spared me and friends who were with me. I felt like this was a sign to stop running from Tyree. We all could have been seriously hurt that day. Running away to one of the women's abuse shelters in South Carolina helped me to discover what religious abuse was. This was a method of abuse I had never heard about. It is when your abuser uses religion to abuse you and make you do what they want you to do by improperly using the Bible. This, among other abuses, is how Tyree was behaving towards me. Many of the things he said or forced me to do were improperly justified by the Bible. When I would leave him, his behavior would escalate. I also would make wrong decisions, doing things I said I would never do. I started feeling like the more I left him, the angrier he would become when I tried to leave him the next time.

During all this "back & forth drama," Kim got pregnant and it upset me when she flaunted it in my face. She was no longer the humble, quiet young girl. This situation reminded me of Rachel and Leah in the Bible. I cared for Kim and she was just as much of a victim as I was. However, at that moment, I was deeply hurt. While she was pregnant, Tyree said he would beat her and even hit her in her stomach. This made me sad for Kim and her baby. She was the only one that I knew about who got pregnant for Tyree. The way Tyree got around there could have been many others. I wanted a child not because of Tyree, but due to my desire to be a mother. Tyree tried to accuse me of being unable to get pregnant. I knew that was his way of trying to justify Kim being pregnant in front of other people who were important to him. He would tell Kim and me that we were his two girls — one big and one skinny. He would say that he could not be with me alone and how he needed someone else just to be with me. He would still cheat on both of us when he was lustful.

As time passed, my family starting questioning Tyree about what he was doing with the property, because many rumors were surfacing about abuse, the church being a cult, and him sleeping with other women living in our home. Tyree was so upset with my family and our neighbors that he started going outside and shooting rounds with his AK rifle early in the morning. He said he wanted to scare people. People would call the cops on him and before you knew it our entire yard would be covered with county police cars. Tyree would talk trash to the police and in return receive pushback. I would stay in the house in fear that something bad was going to happen. He would boast about the police officers being afraid of him. He would not allow them to come into the house to check the property. He acted like he knew his legal rights and the police never confronted him. This situation happened so many times. I was surprised by the response of the police officers. Didn't they know Tyree was an ex–convict? From neighbors' reports, they did know that he was shooting a high–powered gun. The gun shots were so loud!

Tyree said he wanted to make a statement to the neighbors so they would not "fuck" with him. Tyree got his way so much that he apparently believed that he was invincible.

One of the times that I left him for hitting me, I filed a restraining order. Simultaneously, I learned that my mom and my sister Wanda had filed complaints about Tyree abusing me. When I went to court, you could not see any marks on my face because they had cleared up. The judge surprised me and said that if we had a dispute that we could go our separate ways since we both owned the home. What I did not know was when the sheriff delivered the subpoena, Tyree told me that he and Devon were moving the rifle into his truck. He told me that the officer walked up on them and surprised him. What was even more surprising was that he said the officer saw the AK 47 and said nothing to him about the rifle. Nothing! Tyree told me that if that officer had arrested him for possession of that gun, he would have gone to jail for the rest of his life because he was a convicted felon.

I was afraid to seek legal help anymore because I feared for my life and I felt that the law was not trying to protect me. Tyree wanted to build an underground fort on our property. My dad and he got into an altercation over this that resulted in more problems. My dad was a humble man and was not one to start confusion. When Tyree came back home that morning, he told me that he confronted my father for lying about giving me the property. We had to go to court concerning the property, and the judge allowed us to pay rent for it until everything was resolved. Tyree neglected to make the first payment and blamed me, as usual.

I was there in body, but not my mind. The distance between me and my family continued to grow farther apart. Eventually, we had to vacate the land and Tyree moved our mobile home to a trailer park where we rented a lot. Tyree arranged for someone to have the home set up in the trailer park. The person did a botched job and damaged different areas in the interior part of the home. Ultimately, we had to move into the apartment of Tyree's younger sister and her son's father.

Tyree finally applied for a job and resumed working again. He was a janitorial supervisor for a private cleaning company. Devon and Kim also worked for the company and I helped when I could. I knew I could not stay with Tyree.

His mistress, Kim was having his baby and when the pressure got super heavy on me, I decided to pack my belongings in my car trunk without him knowing. After I packed my car, I told him I was leaving him forever. I did not think he would fight me in front of his younger sister and her son's father. When I told him, I was sitting in a chair and Tyree was standing in front of me. Once again, Tyree surprised me when he took his Timberland steel toe boot and kicked me in my face. Before I realized what was happening, he kicked me a second time in my face.

He grabbed me "super fast" by my hair and we struggled while he dragged me down the hallway to the kitchen. Tyree was beating me in my face with his fist.

He held me with one hand and told me he was looking for a knife in the kitchen to cut me. I was screaming at the top of my lungs for help and no one initially got involved. Then, Devon came in and stood — moving from side to side — stunned not knowing what to do. I was kicking Tyree and tried to dig my nails into his jeans to wring his penis. No matter how hard I struggled, I could not grab it. I knew I had to do whatever I could to keep him from finding a knife in that kitchen. So, I kept hitting, kicking, and screaming for help. Thankfully, Tyree's younger sister and her son's father came into the kitchen and separated us. Tyree begged his sister to take me out of the apartment and finish me off, but she was able to calm him down.

He scared me enough to think he would have carried it out if I did not do what he wanted me to do. As previously done, he tried to intimidate me, and it worked.

He once had shot a pistol above my head and had pointed his AK rifle directly at my chest on other occasions. Of all the times he beat me, this time was the worst. He was so angry — calling me "stupid bitch," talking about how he sacrificed so much for me and did all kinds of things for me, and how I was never satisfied.

How crazy it was for him to say he had sacrificed so much, when in fact, it was I who had sacrificed so much! His sister talked him into letting me go. Before I left, his sister gave me a handful of pain reliever pills and told me I would need them the next morning. I did not know how bad my face looked until then.

My face was so bruised and hurting that I could hardly open my eyes or talk.

A chunk of my hair was pulled out and the pain was throbbing all over my body.

I was in pain for days! I called a male friend and colleague, and he came to help me. He was so upset that he wanted me to give him permission to get back at Tyree for what he did to me. I told him, "No!" I have always believed that God has the best way of punishing wrongdoing. When it comes to vengeance, "Vengeance is mine, says the Lord. I will repay."

My male friend & colleague paid for me to stay at a motel for a few days.

I had previously told Tyree about this male friend and

colleague, hoping that Tyree would be jealous of someone else liking me. To my surprise, Tyree encouraged me to date him as if it was a joke. However, this guy was also involved in illegal activity. So, our relationship was short–lived. There was no need for me to involve myself in another unhealthy relationship. In fact, he had a girlfriend and wanted me and her to be with him just like Tyree. I knew that I had made a mistake. It was one that I had to pay for later. When I finally went back to Tyree, he and I cried together after I told him that I was intimate with my male friend & colleague.

Tyree had always threatened me that he would never accept me back if I slept with another guy. Tyree surprised me again and begged me to come back to him. He told me that he forgave me, but he did not live it down. I did not want to keep any secrets, but I wished that I never told him about my affair. He talked about my unfaithfulness every chance he got. Tyree appeared to be happy to have something over my head. Maybe, he did so to make his ill behavior appear justifiable. He acted like he hated me for wanting to do the right thing.

From that point on, every incident got more severe. Somehow, Tyree knew this guy's close family member that was in prison with Tyree. I do not know if someone exposed me and this guy, but Tyree never mentioned to me that he knew him.

It is so ironic that we saw my male friend & colleague so many times after the affair.

When I moved back into Tyree's sister's apartment with him, his sister signaled me to follow her upstairs for what I thought would be a private girl chat that we often had. I did not pay any attention that she did not say a word. When we got into the guest bedroom that Tyree and I occupied, she turned around and spat in my face with a mouth full of liquid. I was upset, but I understood her being angry. How could I have come back to her brother after she had put herself on the line to help me? Maybe, she could have been evicted if someone complained about all the noise that had occurred. I knew I was up this dangerous creek without a paddle.

I do not know what it is about an abusive relationship. You believe, if you support your abuser and love them through the abuse, they will begin behaving in a healthy manner. What we fail to see as a victim that loves them unconditionally is that if that person does not want to change, there is nothing we can do. There is also the possibility that the abuser does not believe that anything is wrong with them. Only God can change someone's heart and mind. If we who have been abused do not recognize this reality during the vicious cycle of abuse, the outcome can be (and has been) fatal. Additionally, when I made the bad decision to be intimate with my guy friend, I did not realize how I was causing self–inflicted pain and hurting more than anyone else involved. All I knew was that my moral upbringing did not teach me to be unfaithful to my husband, but I justified what I did because I had made up my mind to leave Tyree for good. He was the one always cheating on me! When someone hurts you, the pain can cause you to desire wanting them to feel pain too. You do not realize that you are only compounding hurting yourself.

Eventually, Tyree & I moved back to our mobile home. It was still unfinished, but we made it work. It was Tyree's idea for me to resume exercising. He said that I was the biggest woman in the group and the other girls took care of their bodies — implying that I was not taking care of myself. I resumed exercising and it was good for me as I was able to release some of my frustrations. Kim and Devon's girlfriend, Strawberry, were kicked out of the group for disagreeing with Tyree. He informed me that he would make the young people go through initiations, including Strawberry. He did not make me go through it and I remember feeling stunned that he would do that. I never saw what he would make them do. Tyree said this was supposed to be a secret. He told me he made her strip naked, bow down to him, and kiss his feet for her initiation. I knew Tyree wanted to be intimate with Strawberry. She was 17. Devon really loved Strawberry.

Tyree influenced Devon to break up with Strawberry because of her betrayal and Devon did it. He did whatever Tyree told him to do. This was the start of a new relationship for Kim and Strawberry that birthed out of resentment towards Tyree. By this time, Kim had delivered their baby. I remember feeling so nervous inside and afraid of potential gossip. I stopped worrying about getting pregnant and that was when I got pregnant, too. Tyree told me to wait to take a pregnancy test.

I was excited and I knew I had missed my monthly cycle that always came on time. I waited but I knew I would eventually find a way to check. Then, during the next month, I got so sick and could barely hold down any food. At first, I thought I had a stomach virus, but it was happening every day 'til my fourth month of pregnancy.

During this time, there were more people who joined the "church" — more couples than single people. Some of them needed a place to stay so Tyree moved them in with us. He was back on track and found a building to rent for services on Saturdays. The person who owned the building was one of my nail care customers that also owned a radio station and a funeral parlor. This building was used to host viewings before the funeral.

People met by Tyree, who were out in the streets, would come to the "church."

It was good for anyone who needed someplace to belong, but it was bad because Tyree had an ill motive. He still drank alcohol, smoked weed, and was still dipping and dabbling with young girls. These girls that came around to the "church" were naïve about him. People were attracted to him because he spoke about the Bible and spoke eloquently. I acted in my role as "Church Mother" because he forced me, but I did not want to be there. Tyree always talked with bravado and would always want me to back up by saying, "Right, Queen?" As I was tired of hearing his nonsense, I am sure others were too. He lost respect with some of the members because of girls accusing him of flirting and interacting inappropriately with them. He would have bible study and prepare himself for Saturday Sabbath Services. Tyree assigned some of the young men to record his messages. He brought the neighborhood children to "church" and let them hang out weekly at our home to help keep them off the streets. Everybody followed his instructions and looked up to him as their leader no matter what he said or did.

Tyree got in trouble again, one day, for smoking weed while traveling to South Carolina. Devon was with him when they were pulled over by a highway patrolman. Tyree said the officer smelled weed in the car and found paraphernalia in the car. He went to court and was charged a fine that had to be paid by a specific date. He did not have the money to pay it, so he was issued an arrest warrant. Shortly thereafter, our electricity was shut off in our mobile home. One day while sleeping, I heard the children outside. They were teasing and throwing rocks at our Rottweiler's face. Some of these children were notorious for being bad and occasionally not listening. We stopped them from coming over to the house because they could not play the video games without electricity. I opened the door and told them to leave the dog alone. The dog could not move anywhere because we had him tied up. When I went back inside, the kids started laughing loudly. I could hear the rocks hitting the side of the mobile home. I woke Tyree up and told him what the kids were doing. Tyree put on some shoes and said he was going to take care of this. He ran outside the door behind the children with a belt. I put on shoes and ran behind him. I saw him running behind one of the kids, while she was on her bike. He used the belt to scare them off, but the situation blew up because he hit one of the kids on the leg with the belt. I knew this child's mother because she had been a prior nail care customer. While we were taking care of these children — feeding them and allowing them to play at our home — their parents never had a problem. This mother had given us permission, in front of a group of people, to spank her children if they were disrespectful. No one ever scolded them until this day.

The girl that Tyree hit with the belt yelled that she was going to tell her mom.

She did not cry in front of us; but when she got home, she started crying and holding her leg as if she had been beaten severely. Tyree and I looked at each other with amazement! The mother told Tyree that she was calling the cops and did not want to listen to anything he had to say. He pleaded with me to talk to the mom while he took off running. He told me that he would go to jail if the cops arrested him. This mother told the cops what her daughter had said about Tyree spanking her.

I defended him and told them that it was me. Tyree told me that they would not do anything to me. I knew the cops wanted Tyree instead and they probably checked the house to see if he was there. I could not believe it when the cop said he was arresting me. Why should I or anyone get arrested for spanking a child for misbehaving, especially when you were trying to protect the child from stirring up a Rottweiler? They asked me about Tyree, and I would not give them any information. I am sure the officer who questioned me was upset, which was followed by him handcuffing me. I knew Tyree was emotionally imbalanced, but what he did that day was innocently trying to stop the children from getting hurt.

He was not trying to hurt any of the children with the belt — just scare them.

After the officer handcuffed me, the girl and the other kids that were bothering the dog was sitting on the steps of the girl's house making faces at me. They started licking their tongues and laughing at me as I sat in the patrol car. I told Tyree that

I did not want to be bothered with these kids. He was the one that said the kids did not have anything to do around the park and he wanted to help them. What if the dog had got a hold on and bit one of them? It would have been terrible! When I went before the judge for my bond hearing, I was released on my own recognizance and given a court hearing date. Tyree sent Devon to pick me up and we went back to the trailer. It was trashed like someone was looking for something. Tyree said he did not know if the cops did it or not. He said we could not stay there. So, he took me to the house of a lady that I realized I also knew. He claimed that he slept with her to get money from her for my bail. We were also dealing with the possibility of losing our home. We had payments and fees that had accumulated and had no way of paying them. It was only a matter of time before the creditors mandated the overdue payments. At that point, I was detached from the home and did not care if we lost it. I was tired of running away. I just wanted to be stable, pray, and talk to God about what to do. Tyree told me he had made some arrangements with the lady who owned the mobile home park to keep our home. We owed her so much rent, anyway.

Tyree retained his cleaning job and I had been servicing nail care customers, but he was not willing to change his bad habits of drinking and smoking weed.

My car payments were also overdue, and I knew it was only a matter of time before it would be repossessed.

One of my nail care customers and I were talking one day about Tyree and my urgent need to find a place to stay. She surprised me and extended an invitation to Tyree and me to stay in her home. She knew I was pregnant and did not want to see us homeless. We moved in before my court date. It was a two–bedroom trailer and both sides had rooms with full bathrooms and the rooms were spacious and fully furnished. It seemed bigger inside than the outside. She and her husband fed us and treated us with kindness. She did not ask us to pay any rent.

She just wanted to see us recover from this setback. My nail care customer began taken a liking to Tyree because he would buy her marijuana and spend time talking to her. They both liked to talk at length. She was an older lady, but she still enjoyed smoking her cigarettes and marijuana. When it was time for me to go to court,

I had to go alone because Tyree still had an outstanding arrest warrant.

When I arrived in court, the police officer approached me asking questions about Tyree, and I refused to give him any information. The officer asked the judge to confer the maximum penalty. Though pregnant, I did not make it known. I thought by the time I served my sentence I would be fine. I was sentenced to a maximum of

30 days. The officer did not charge me with Tyree's crime because he still wanted Tyree to pay for what happened, but he charged me for false information. Immediately following the court hearing, I was taken to jail. I was afraid of going to jail and I did not know what to expect. I kept to myself and did not say much to anyone. I had a chance to reflect on everything that had taken place. I spent about two weeks in jail and then was released early for working and good behavior.

I praised God! It was strange because I felt like I was coming back to jail, like God was preparing me for what was soon to come. However, I pushed back the thought in my spirit. I wanted to get away as far as I could from that jailhouse, so I started walking and got a ride the rest of the way. I did not call Tyree because I wanted to surprise him and see what he was up to. When I arrived at my friend's home, she greeted me with a hug and told me how happy she was to see me. Tyree was fast asleep in bed. He looked like a wild man with his long dreadlocks and unshaved face. When he saw me, he looked like he had seen a ghost. He mentioned to me that my friend's home was like a hideaway for him and he did not want to bring anyone around. I asked him again if I could go see an obstetrician, and he said, "No." I thought, Why not?!...

"We are troubled on every side, yet not distressed;
we are perplexed, but not in despair;
Persecuted, but not forsaken; cast down, but not destroyed;
For which cause we faint not; but though our outward
man perish, yet the inward man is renewed day by day.
For our light affliction, which is but for a moment, worketh
for us a far more exceeding and eternal weight of glory;
While we look not at the things which are seen, but at the
things which are not seen: for the things which are seen are
temporal; but the things which are not seen are eternal."

2 Corinthians 4:8–9, 16–18 (NKJV)

CHAPTER 4

❧

FALSELY ARRESTED

IT WAS 2002 when Tyree decided he was ready to see his newborn daughter. He told me that he wanted me to be the mother of Kim's baby and for the baby to call me mom. I did not want nor was it right to take Kim's place with her child. He wanted me to contact her and ask her about him being able to see the baby. Our circle became small and included Devon, his younger sister, and his sister's boyfriend. During my pregnancy, I had cravings for Taco Bell.

I had to sneak there because Tyree did not want me to eat meat, just seafood. I knew Strawberry used to work there, but the times that I went there, she was off shift. I thought maybe she had quit. When I finally crossed paths with Strawberry, I did not know if she would greet me. Surprisingly, she hugged me and spoke kindly. I was happy because I liked Strawberry. She said that she missed everyone, but deeply disliked Tyree and said so adamantly. Something happened between her and Tyree. Maybe, they had an affair, but I can only speculate. It was the tone in her voice that made me feel that way. Hell has no fury like a woman scorned and

I knew from our conversation that she deeply resented him. She told me that she would bring Kim to meet with me. We all met and talked. Kim decided she would bring the baby to see him. She seemed like she was excited to come, and I am sure she wanted her child to know her father. When Tyree decided on a time, he sent his sister and me to the house of Kim's mother to pick them up. Tyree told me to tell my friend & her husband, in whose home we were staying, that Kim was his cousin. He did not want my friend & her husband to know the truth about what he was doing.

Devon resumed being involved with Strawberry again unbeknownst to Tyree. When Tyree found out, he was upset. Kim and the baby came over and the baby had tight rubber bands in her hair. You could see that the baby's scalp was red and irritated. Tyree told Kim not to let anyone put rubber bands in the baby's hair again. He took them out the baby's hair. Then, the next time that he saw Kim and the baby, there were rubber bands in the baby's hair again. This made Tyree furious toward Kim. Kim said it was Strawberry who put the rubber bands back in the baby's hair. I prayed to God to help me get out of the ongoing situational drama. Fervently and from the depths of my heart, I asked God to take Tyree completely out of my life. I began having this heavy unsettled feeling in my heart like something horrible was going to happen to me. I told Tyree about dreaming this, but he told me he did not want to hear anything I had to say.

The majority of my dreams were about pending confusion. However, this one was about a death angel around me. I did not know what was going to happen or who it was going to be, but I prayed for God to have mercy. The feeling came over me so strong that I would cry. I did not want Tyree to hit me and cause any problems for my pregnancy. So I refrained from expressing this sadness.

Kim and the baby had come over again and she was emotionally upset. Her family had been saying mean things to her concerning Tyree and the baby. I am sure Strawberry also had something to say. I told Tyree to let Kim go back home, but she cried and begged him to allow her and the baby to stay. For that night, she and the baby stayed with us. The next day, January 8, 2002, Tyree and I went to wash clothes at the laundry mat. While we were washing clothes, he was on the phone with multiple members of Kim's family. They were going back and forth about the baby. I was still traveling doing manicures for extra money and had some customers that afternoon. When we got back from the laundry mat, I was running late to a customer's home. I remember the look on Tyree's face when I left. He looked confused, and I remember feeling that I was not going to see him again. It was a strange feeling that ran through me. It was like time had slowed down for a moment. I still sensed a strong feeling of death, but what could I do?

When I left, my friend and her husband were home along with Tyree, Kim, and the baby. When I arrived at my manicure customer/friend's home where I was supposed to meet another manicure customer, the customer had not yet arrived.

We had been trying to reach her and left voicemails. For whatever reason, the phone lines were acting crazy that afternoon. There had to have been something wrong at a town in South Carolina that day because we had never had this problem. When my customer finally called back, it was hours later and close to the time for my next appointment across town. She said she would just reschedule since it was so late. So, I packed my manicure items back in my car. I was disappointed and hoping to make some money because I was nearly broke. I had not eaten anything all day and my gas tank was nearly empty. With the money I had ($4.00), I was going to figure out how to get something to eat. Tyree finally told me a few days prior that I could see an obstetrician.

I called the house to check on everyone, while I was driving to my next appointment, but no one answered their phones. My friend had two house phones and Kim and Tyree had cell phones. I still sensed that strong, sad feeling of death and decided to go check on them before my next customer appointment.

When I drove toward our residence, I noticed two police cars in the driveway.

So, I passed by instead of pulling up. I figured I would just call them back to find out what happened. Tyree always had a way of talking himself out of things with the police. I was worried, but not enough to stop and find out what was going on. I tried to call everyone at our residence to no avail. I left voicemails to inform them that I saw police cars outside and was asking them if everything was alright.

Through some delayed signal relay, I finally saw that Tyree tried to call me, but the call kept dropping. I stopped at a pay phone to try to reach them and someone finally answered. Tyree answered and told me he had been shot.

I dropped to my knees. All kinds of emotions rushed through my mind.

At that moment, I saw police cars driving across town at high speeds. Oh My God! I was so scared and nervous! He said the cops came in the house and he got shot.

I did not know the details of what happened, but I was afraid for him.

Whatever the outcome, I would not have to worry about this man abusing me anymore. I knew he had an outstanding warrant, so he would finally be arrested!

He did not mention if everyone else at the residence was alright. I was deeply concerned! So, I began to head back to our residence.

While I was driving towards our residence, I saw more cop cars driving pass me at high speeds. I remember feeling that Tyree would not live through this.

The closer I got to our residence, the more cops I saw along with other cars stopped on the highway. People were standing outside of their cars to see what was happening. I found a place off the road to park my car so I could also see what was going on. The closer I got, I could see many police officers standing around.

One male officer was pushing a person that was lying on the ground, in their back with his foot. The person appeared to be Tyree, who did not seem to be awake.

I screamed out afraid, "Wait! That is my husband!" I

held my stomach and ran down to them! Three male officers stopped me and said that I could not come any closer. Some of them were in civilian clothes and some were in uniforms.

I told them that I needed to know what was going on with my husband and asked if he was alright. One of the officers in civilian clothes told me, that if I did not calm down, he was going to arrest me for public disorderly conduct.

Then, an ambulance arrived on the scene and I asked again about Tyree.

They started questioning me about Tyree and my relationship with him. I got scared, denied that he was my husband, and said he was just some guy with whom I had a relationship. I did not know what condition he was in, but I knew that it did not look good at all. I was praying for him to survive. I wanted him to get locked up but not die.

I continued asking questions about Tyree and the same officer that told me to calm down said he was going to lock me up. He put my hands behind my back, and this made it uncomfortable for me to breathe. Though I told him that I was pregnant, and he was able to see my physical condition, he did not care.

The officer made me wait in his patrol car until a female officer arrived to escort me to the detention center. In this moment, it was harder for me to catch my breath with my hands tied behind my back. The officer informed me that I was going to be held for public disorderly conduct. I remember the last time Tyree got me into trouble, and this time I was not trying to get in trouble for him or anyone else. Besides, I was more concerned about my unborn baby than myself. The police officer mentioned to me that two officers were "down."

I was praying that these officers would survive this ordeal. When the female officer finally arrived, she and a male officer drove me to a South Carolina Sheriff Department.

I was still having a hard time with breathing and I asked them to call an ambulance for me. They reluctantly did not rush to call the ambulance as if they did not believe me. When the EMTs arrived, I was given a bag to breathe through until

I could breathe better. After sitting for a long while, a male detective of Asian descent, introduced himself and asked if I wanted to give a statement. I replied, "Not without an attorney." Then he asked me if I would write a statement. I again replied, "Not without an attorney." He said to me, "You know that's impossible."

I shrugged my shoulders at him. I thought, "Why would this be impossible according to Miranda Rights?" He turned to the male officer that brought me in and instructed the officer to take me to the detention center. The male officer told him that he was not my arresting officer. He said for him to take me down, anyway. The male officer asked him, "What should be the booking charge?"

The detective replied, "Book her for public disorderly conduct."

So, I was arrested after refusing to be questioned without an attorney present. No Miranda Rights were read to me. I was just escorted by the male and female officer to a County Detention Center for Public Disorderly Conduct with handcuffs on my hands behind my back. When I was asked my name, I told them "Nzuri." I was fingerprinted, my picture was taken, and personal belongings were confiscated.

Then, they gave me one of those orange jumpsuits to put on and locked me into a disgusting jail cell. After being there for a while, a female SLED agent came into the cell to test my hands for lead. I knew from crime drama television shows that when you are tested for lead, you are being checked for gun powder residue.

I knew that I had not shot a gun but she tested me, anyways. I was not at the crime scene when the crime was committed or anytime afterwards. So, I initially refused to give her my hands to test. She told me that they could make me. All I could imagine is these officers holding me down with my baby in my stomach. I was afraid of what would happen, so I gave in to the test. I knew they were not going to find anything and that is what I told her.

I asked for a phone call when everything calmed down; and the Correctional Officer, at the time, granted my request. Though I felt awkward, I called my mother so I could be the first to tell her where I was. My mother's first response was,

"Did you call the police about a domestic disturbance?" I responded. "No."

I told her that I did not know much about the situation. She said that she would give our attorney friend a call. After returning to my jail cell, I saw Devon come in with handcuffs on. He had bandages wrapped around his hands. He said that he was with his dad when officers came and arrested him from a store. He said they brought him in on false information charges. The female SLED agent returned asking the detention center officers for my phone, purse, clothes, and shoes.

They wanted to take them to the lab. I told her that she could not have them until

I spoke to an attorney, but nobody paid attention to what I said.

Later, I received a visit from the detention center's head nurse, Ms. Campbell and her assistant nurse. They wanted to talk with me.

They started out with general questions and then started interrogating me with questions including, Are you using drugs? Did you receive prenatal care for your baby? How far along are you? She told me that if I was not receiving prenatal care that I could be charged with child neglect. Nurse Campbell also said that she was going to call child welfare services. She and her assistant left the jail cell to make phone calls. When she came back to the jail cell, she told me that because

I was only in my second trimester, there was nothing that could be done to me. Then, Nurse Campbell and her assistant said that I was acting like I was on drugs. So, they made me take a urine test which I did with no problem. They asked if I was using alcohol. I replied, "No." They told me that I could get my child taken away from me. After they took my urine sample, Nurse Campbell and her assistant did not come back with the results. They came back to ask me more questions, including "Do you have any suicidal thoughts?" I replied, "Absolutely Not!"

Then, they said that I needed to talk with a therapist, as if I was some crazed woman that needed to calm down or was on the verge of a nervous breakdown. In this moment, I felt like they were profiling me as someone who was emotionally and/or mentally unstable. Nothing could be farther from the truth. Next, they placed me in a one–person holding cell by the nurses' desk. There was a camera in the cell.

I made up the bed and sat down. My heart was racing from all the drama of the day. I could feel my baby putting pressure on my bladder. I did not want to lose my baby, so I was determined to focus on calming thoughts. I asked the officers if I could have something to eat because I had not yet eaten. The officers said that the kitchen was closed. I was so exhausted! So I laid down on the cot and went to sleep.

Early the next morning, an inmate came to the nurses' station to get his medication. He told the overnight nurse, Ms. Taylor, that the guy who was accused of killing two cops was dead. I got so scared that I ran to the jail cell door and asked the inmate to please repeat what he said. He said to me, "Oh, you that girl! I don't know nothing! I don't know nothing." I begged him crying and said, "Please, please tell me what you just told the nurse?" He and Nurse Taylor just looked at me with a crazy stare. Shortly afterwards, inmates were delivering breakfast trays. I got out of the bed — still crying from hearing that Tyree had died and knowing I had to eat something for my baby. As I was eating, two SLED agents came to the nurses' station with papers in their hands looking for Nzuri. I could see Nurse Taylor pointing toward me. I was thinking that they were coming to tell me that Tyree was dead. I asked them their names and they told me. Then they started reading a document that said I was being arrested for two counts of accessory to murder. What?! I had not committed any kind of crime! Then, I cheered up because they mentioned that Tyree was being charged with two counts of murder.

I knew that they could not charge a dead man, so that meant he was still alive.

A few hours later, I was told to get ready for a legal visit. The first thought that came to mind was that the detectives were coming back to harass me, like in certain crime drama movies. To my surprise, it was the attorney friend that my mom called. He came to check on me and said that he would be my legal representation. It was so nice to see a familiar face. After talking with my family's attorney friend, I went back to the jail cell to wait for a bond hearing. I hoped that the bond would be as it was when James got me in trouble. I recognized the two SLED agents who came earlier to see me were present at the bond hearing, along with my attorney. After the judge read all three charges, she asked me if I had any questions. I looked at my attorney then the judge and replied, "Not at this time." Then she turned to the two SLED agents who represented the state for their response. They requested that I be "held without bond" until they completed their investigation. The judge denied my bond and I was escorted back to the medical holding cell. The female correctional officer instructed me to gather my belongings. Then, she escorted me to a one–person holding cell in front of the booking desk. They wanted me to be on a 24–hour suicide watch and the lights stayed on for an entire week.

Shortly after the bond hearing, I was escorted to the Magistrate's Court by the same female officer for my misdemeanor charge of public disorderly conduct. I had already requested that my attorney file for a jury trial because I was not going to plead guilty for something I did not do.

While being on suicide watch, they refused to let me make phone calls to anyone including my attorney.

I complained about how unfair that was and how they were violating my civil rights. The nurses came in periodically to check on me and the chaplain came in to see if I wanted to talk. He brought me some reading material and I thanked him.

I was not allowed to take showers for the entire week. As the week passed, I got a huge headache from the lights being on all day and night. When I asked for them to be turned off, my request was denied. The correctional officers told me that they were not allowed to turn off the lights because I was on suicide watch.

Some officers refused to let me read the newspaper so I could know what was going on with my case.

When Monday came, they took me off suicide watch. An officer escorted me to the pod where all the female inmates were housed. When I first entered the pod, a short Caucasian female officer called me to her desk. She whispered to me not to talk to anyone about what was going on with my case because there were numerous inmates looking to "cut deals." On this day, I finally had a chance to make calls, watch the news, and read the newspaper. I was placed in a one–person cell on the first floor of a two–story pod. I was (6) months pregnant and sleeping on a steel bed with a thin pad as a mattress. It was miserable, but I finally was able to take a shower! This pod was much cleaner than the holding cells by the front entrance of the detention center. I was informed not to climb the stairs because I was pregnant. This was a problem because the visitation area and the laundry room were on the 2nd floor.

My case made the front page of the newspaper, sold out newspapers, and was broadcast via t.v. news for many weeks. I remembered reading and hearing people talk daily about this tragedy. They would reference Tyree first and then me.

The Sheriff's Department defamed my character and that angered me.

They miscommunicated to the public that I was the one who made the 911 phone call, and was the person trying to help Tyree escape from the crime scene.

It was Tyree's mistress, Kim who was with Tyree when he escaped from the scene.

Additionally, Strawberry was the one who called the police who responded which then resulted in the shootout. These were the facts.

*"When the enemy comes in like a flood, the Spirit of
the Lord shall lift up a standard against him."*
Isaiah 59:19b (NKJV)

CHAPTER 5

❧

COURT AND INCARCERATION

Preliminary Hearing

APPROXIMATELY TWO MONTHS had passed since my incarceration and it was now time for my preliminary hearing. Now, I was (8) months pregnant. My parents were able to secure (2) criminal attorneys for me. One of my attorneys, Mr. Hart, suggested that no public appearance for me. He wanted me to waive my rights to appear in court. They were also working on separating Tyree's case from mine, which eventually happened. I told Mr. Hart that there was no way I was going to waive my rights to appear in court. I also expressed to him that the Sheriff's Department suppressed the fact that I was (6) months pregnant when they arrested me.

So, I wanted the public to see exactly what was going on. Mr. Hart also asked me to cut my locks. I told Mr. Hart that it was not an option. I also expressed to him that I would never be able to change the color of my skin. I told both of my attorneys, Mr. Hart and Mr. Chaplin, that God is my judge and I have done nothing wrong! They both openly expressed to me that I was being falsely accused and they knew that I wanted to sue the County Sheriff's Department for what they were doing to me and my unborn child. They would always say to me do not mention the lawsuit to anyone until my case was over. Mr. Chaplin would say, "If it ain't broke, don't try to fix it." In other words, they did not want me to add any more pressure to the case while it was in progress. I listened and followed their guidance, but I was angry at this point and was going to deliver my baby soon!

On the day of my preliminary hearing, my attorneys visited me to give an overview of the hearing process. When I returned to my cell, I remained there until a transportation officer came to escort me to court. Currently, Tyree's preliminary case was in progress. I was escorted to a smaller courtroom nearby to await my hearing. Mr. Hart came to see me and reminded me to not make eye contact or wave to anyone, including family and friends. Thirty minutes later, someone came into where I and the transportation officer were waiting to escort me into the courtroom. The officer took me to the General Sessions courtroom door and pointed to where my attorneys were. As I walked over to my attorneys, I looked up to a packed-out court room. To my surprise, most people were family and friends. I was so happy to see my parents sitting right behind the table where my attorneys and I were sitting! I also deeply appreciated all the support by others who cared about me! I strolled in slowly (as my attorney had instructed me) and held my belly, as I walked through the courtroom. I started feeling shortness of breath from being so nervous. I took my seat between my attorneys. I observed that the courtroom was filled with news reporters and cameras snapping photos of me.

Mr. Hart was first with his opening remarks. One of the major points Mr. Hart talked about was the three factors for my charges which included two counts of "accessory to murder after the fact." He pointed out to SLED agent Avant, who testified on behalf of the state and was the leading SLED agent on my case that for me to be charged, I had to have either aided or abetted, harbored, and/or assisted Tyree (who was the principal defendant). So, Mr. Hart asked SLED agent Avant how I did any of these things. The response by SLED agent Avant was based on speculation not actuality. Mr. Hart noted this and stated that the principal (Tyree) had already been apprehended before I arrived on the scene. Mr. Chaplin asked later, "Why wasn't Kimberly, the person seen with Tyree while and after the shooting took place, arrested and charged?" Mr. Avant's response was, "Because she was the victim." It was also brought up that Ms. Blake had lied in her first statement, and she is supposed to be a witness for the state to corroborate that he made phone calls and that I was one of the people called.

Ms. Blake also has a (7) month–old baby by Mr. Roberts.

I was still being held "without bond" and my case had returned what is called a "true bill" from the grand jury. A "true bill" is "a written decision, handed down by a grand jury, that the evidence presented by the prosecution is sufficient to believe that the accused person likely committed the crime and should be indicted." The solicitor told the judge, during my preliminary hearing, that there was no need to make a ruling. I did not understand all that was being said.

Why were my charges not being dismissed so I could go home and deliver my baby in a healthy environment? My attorneys informed me that the court already knew my case was coming back with a "true bill" from the grand jury and that the preliminary hearing was just a formality. My attorneys told me that they were going to ask for a 2nd bond hearing. I was happy that the truth about this dramatic & tragic situation was being brought to light!

At the same time, I was deeply saddened by the obstinate behavior of staff in the County Sheriff's Department. I was told that due to the inaccurate portrayal of me to the public, there were multiple threats of injury and death toward me. I was afraid for my unborn child, my parents, and myself. What if some crazy person decided to open fire on my family or a cop went rogue and sought revenge on my family? The Sheriff's Department and everyone else involved left me open to people hating me for no legitimate reason. I tried to push the issue hard with my attorneys in preparation for a 2nd bond hearing. It seemed like the process was taking so long. I hoped that the court would extend compassion and at least let me go home to deliver my baby, even if it meant me wearing a house arrest ankle bracelet. I did not mind at all. I could not fathom the thought of being separated from my child. After all, I did not do anything wrong. Why should my baby have to suffer too?

*"No weapon formed against you shall prosper; and every tongue
which rises against you in judgment you shall condemn.
This is the heritage of the servants of the Lord, and
their righteousness is from Me, says the Lord."*
Isaiah 54:17 (NKJV)

*Many are the afflictions of the righteous,
But the Lord delivers him out of them all.*
Psalms 34:19 (NKJV)

Bond Hearing

My bond hearing was to be set up after my preliminary hearing. The nurses and I had become cordial with each other because I had to see them every day.

It was their job to make sure I had my prenatal vitamins and anything else related to my pregnancy. Nurse Campbell and her assistant mentioned that they were going to advocate for me to be granted a bond so I could go home and give birth to my baby. She said that sometimes the judge would use their opinion of what should be done with a patient. I was surprised, happy, and expressed my gratitude for their willingness to speak up for me. I mentioned what they said to my attorneys.

Closer to my bond hearing, Nurse Campbell and her assistant came to me while I was in the recreation yard. They asked if I had anyone willing to bail me out if a bond were set so that I could go home. They told me that they did not want to deal with my pregnancy because "Common Sense. If anything were to happen to you and the baby, it would be on the County Detention Center."

Nurse Campbell said at this time, they did not want to risk it. So, to answer the nurses' question about the bond, I told them "Yes, I believe that my family would be willing to help in any way possible." In other words, Nurse Campbell and her assistant were all for letting me go home to deliver my baby.

Approximately one to two weeks later, Nurse Campbell came to the women's pod to tell me, "Mr. Fitzgibbons, the Director, told me that I don't have to go to court on your behalf and there's not a damn thing that anyone could do about that!"

I informed my attorneys of what she said. When it was time for me to go to court, Nurse Campbell changed her attitude towards me like night and day! Mr. Hart told me not to worry about it and that they had issued a subpoena to her. There was also a written statement from my doctor, Dr. Washington, stating the importance of a child's early stage of life, especially the bonding between child and mother.

My attorneys emphasized the health issue regarding me nursing my baby and how this would be County Detention Center's first experience with a woman giving birth while incarcerated at their facility. My attorneys adamantly expressed that they did not want me to be a case study, and how I would wear a house arrest ankle bracelet if needed. Mr. Murdough, the solicitor, got up to say that my living conditions were not livable, along with stating other points.

Mrs. Tate, one of the widows of the fallen officers, passionately stated that she did not believe that I should have a right to go home because I was just as much at fault as Tyree. She also stated that she would feel unsafe for her and her children if I was released on bond. I received no remorse from her or the state. So, the judge said that since I was living in bad conditions, I was grown, and no one could tell me what to do even if I was going to live with my parents (as my attorneys aforementioned to the court). So, Judge Gregory said that was my problem.

Then, the judge asked if a court date had been set yet. No response was given to the judge from the solicitor. The judge decided "bond is denied" and that he would reconsider in a few months if my case was not brought forward by a certain time. Once again, I felt so disappointed and hurt! This bond denial was another rude awakening about how politically tied my case was.

Now I had to prepare for the nightmare reality that was soon to take place in my life and my unborn child's life. GOD, please help us!!! What more could I do or say? I wanted to scream!!! I could not believe my ears and the scene from the courtroom. If I were guilty of a crime, I could understand the ill feelings, but it is totally different when you know you are innocent and you are emotionally suffering trying to prove your innocence. To add insult to injury, my child is mixed up in this foolishness! I felt so lifeless and alone. I believe that my attorneys tried to do the best that they could, or did they? All I knew was that God had His eyes on my situation, and I was confident that God was going to have the last say.

I would be lying if I said that I did not ask, "Why God?!" This craziness happened because two young girls got caught up with this dangerous man and did not realize that he was not playing games. Now, lives have been lost and lives are being destroyed. On the flip side, I primarily blamed Tyree for making our lives a Living Hell!!! He used me, Kim, Strawberry, and anyone else who he could manipulate and control for his ill & selfish benefit. He took all of us for granted and did not care about our feelings. Now Kim, I, and our children were stuck in this court system —fighting for our lives. Where was Strawberry when all of this was going on? Initially, I and Kim went through repeated abuse from this man and now we could be separated from our children.

After the 2nd bond hearing, reality kicked in and I could feel it in the pit of my soul. I held myself up long enough to go to the cell so I could cry alone and talk with God. I told God that I believe that anything is possible with Him and

I will keep hope alive, but if the worst was going to happen then please prepare me. Even then I could not imagine being separated from my first child.

I was a first-time mother and thought, "Oh God! Please let this burden pass by me!" I knew about hideous things that had happened to people, but nothing could have prepared me for this. What could I do? I was completely defenseless and emotionally hurting deeply. I rubbed my belly and cried myself to sleep.

The next day I awoke and spoke to the Lord and asked what He wanted me to learn from this situation. I reset my attitude and did my best to rest in

His Perfect Peace. I knew that I needed to avoid being stressed out because it would not be good for my unborn child. There would be times when I looked around in that jail cell and it would feel like the walls were caving in. I would close my eyes and pray to God to help me keep a positive mindset. It was hard at times when I was so mad, but I would pick up my Bible and read the word of God. This brought so much peace when I felt I was about to lose my mind!

A few days later, I had a dream that God gave my baby back to me, but the baby was not a newborn. Rather, my baby appeared to be 3 – 4 months old.

This dream gave me hope where there was no hope — to be released, go home, and be with my child. I tried to stay in the cell to refrain from being around females with negative attitudes, mad at the world, and ready to pop at any minute.

I think the only factor keeping everyone incarcerated calm

& cool was them knowing that, if any problems occurred, it could make things worse for their case. Yet, there are still some who do not care about that. So many people were just waiting for months, most of the time, for their cases to go to court. I witnessed so many women giving up, even if they claimed innocence, because they wanted to go home or they wanted to save their jobs, families, or whatever kind of life they had before they were incarcerated. This always made me sad because they believed that the only way out was to "plea bargain." Many people had to deal with a public defender. Public Defenders were overworked state attorneys who could not care about your case, even if they wanted. Additionally, they would also work with the solicitor to convince you that taking a "plea bargain" was the best option to regain your freedom. What they did not tell you was that if you were depending on government services, like housing, SNAP benefits, or Medicaid, you would no longer be eligible for those services because you would be a convicted felon. I am so deeply thankful to God for how He blessed me with loving parents and family members that did not give up on me. The difficult flip side of this was waiting for long periods of time without hearing anything from my attorneys or the court.

An additional fact about being in a pod full of women was hormonal changes with attitudes. I remember one situation that threatened my baby's life involving this girl named Leslie. Leslie was known to be this biggity individual of the pod. She constantly stirred up confusion and stayed on "lock down."

On this particular day, Leslie was trying to take advantage of the oldest, smallest, and nicest officer in the detention center. I was given permission by the night officer, before she got off shift in the morning, to put my name on the list to do laundry. However, she forgot to pass it on to the next officer. I explained to the morning officer what was promised to me, so she allowed me to go to the washer first while Leslie was asleep in her cell. Right before my clothes finished, Leslie woke up and started ranting and raging, asking whose clothes were in the washer. I told her it was mine. We were not allowed to be up on the 2nd floor where the washer was unless we had permission to be there to use it. Well, her bag was already up there so she went to the washer and threatened to remove my clothes from the washer. I told the C.O. that it was not fair, and she tried to tell Leslie to leave them alone. I tried to tell her that the clothes would be finished soon, but Leslie refused to calm down. So, I went to the washer and told her to leave my clothes alone. She got in my face and I knew neither of us wanted more time, but I was not willing to underestimate what she may do. I kept silent and prayed in my heart as she repeatedly said, "Whatcha gonna do, Nzuri? Whatcha gonna do?" The C.O. was unable to control Leslie, so she called for backup.

I kept my cool because I was standing next to the stair rails on the 2nd floor, surrounded by cement floors. Even if I won this fight, my child's life would be at risk. I did not want to lose my child, but Leslie seemed to not back down.

I was not going to let her mishandle me neither. Before I could turn around, I heard the commotion of several officers running into the pod and telling every inmate to return to their cells!

Leslie got put on "lock down." A couple of months later she apologized to me. She was released but got arrested again on some other charges while I was still there.

"And Moses said to the people,
Do not be afraid. Stand still, and see the salvation of
the Lord, which He will accomplish for you today.
For the Egyptians whom you see today, you
shall see again no more forever.
The Lord will fight for you, and you shall hold your peace."

Exodus 14:13–14

CHAPTER 6

✧

DELIVERING HALLELUYAH

AFTER THE CONFRONTATION with Leslie, I was moved into the medical pod.

Nurse Campbell said she did not want anything happening to me and my baby.

I was so sad about being moved into the medical pod because I would be the only female inmate there. I had been actively working out every day in the recreation yard, which was easily accessible in the women's pod. Yet, when I was moved,

I had to make an uneasy adjustment to exercise. Lt. Harley promised that I would get an hour for recreational time each day, but it did not happen. She explained to me that I had to go to the recreation yard closer to the medical department.

I did not know there was one near there. The yard was so small, and you could hardly see the sunlight. This lack of easy access to exercise was so disappointing!

I really wanted to continue exercising to help my body get in shape for the delivery of my baby. As an alternative to exercising in the recreation yard, I asked if I could walk around the nurses' station in the presence of the staff. Thankfully, they said "yes." Every day that I could, I walked. My days turned into nights and my nights turned into days. I woke early before sunrise to pray and I prayed 3 times a day.

I also started to read Scriptures all night (including directly to my unborn child) and would sleep throughout the day — waking only to eat, use the bathroom, and take daily vitamins.

I wore the bright orange jump suit during my entire pregnancy. Going to doctor visits was a chore. I had to swallow my pride just to get through the humiliation and embarrassment. Everywhere I went, I was escorted through the back doors except for the place where my lab work was done. I was shackled from my hands to my feet until about two weeks from my due date. I had to climb two flights of stairs to get to my OB doctor. I was so afraid that I would stumble, fall, and hurt my baby! Even more infuriating, this office building had elevators but because I was an "inmate" I was not allowed to use them. This made me feel like a slave. I had been a popular nail technician in a County for (7) years, with customers from a wide demographic area. Many of them worked at healthcare facilities. Interestingly, my mother worked with my doctor at this clinic months earlier. Everyone at this clinic had a look of pity on their faces when they saw me.

Sadly, they did not know the daunting truth of my story.

My due date was April 15th, which was "Income Tax Filing Day." On April 12th, I went to my regular check–up and my OB doctor discovered that I had dilated to a tight (3) centimeters and asked me if I had experienced any cramping. I replied, "No." Now, there were two officers vs. one taking me to my doctor appointments. My OB doctor told them to check me in at a Memorial Hospital. Simultaneously, I was nervous and scared because I was going to deliver my baby soon! My OB doctor called ahead to the hospital to inform the head nurse to expect me. The nurse registered me as "Nzuri" (as it was on my driver's license) and connected me to a baby monitor to check for contractions. When we arrived, they had me sit in a wheelchair and the two officers rolled me to the Labor & Delivery Department. Once again, I felt so embarrassed having this bright orange jump suit on that got so much attention. People were staring at me, like those at the clinic, with pity and sorrow. I am sure some of them may have wondered,

"Why was a pregnant woman incarcerated?" My mom had been employed in this hospital department for many years. She was the head nurse of the labor & delivery department at one time. The officer was pushing my wheelchair so fast that my entire body was cold from the air. Once we made it to the registration desk, the registrar began to inquire and enter my personal information into the computer database so that I would be all set before admission to deliver my baby. Once again, I was registered under the name "Nzuri." Then the officers rolled me into the labor & delivery room to be connected to the baby monitor. The nurse was cordial and explained what to expect regarding the process for my real–time delivery.

When she strapped me to the monitor, she discovered that I was having light contractions. Shortly afterwards, my doctor came in and did a check–up.

He assessed that I would most likely be back in (72) hours. So, my OB doctor instructed the nurse to discharge me. He also communicated instructions to the correctional officers which needed to be given to the detention center nurses.

When we returned to the detention center, the staff at the detention center seemed to be nervous and edgy. They all knew that I would soon be giving birth to my child. Additionally, the fact remained that I was going to make history by being the first woman to deliver a baby in their care. Knowing this fact made me want to vomit. Prior to going to the hospital, I had been waiting to hear back from Mr. Foot, the Detention Center Deputy Director, to give me a decision about my request to allow my parents to accompany me for my baby's delivery. In my request,

I emphasized that I would deeply appreciate having my parents with me to support my child's birth. I did not want to be alone. Surprisingly, Mr. Foot took time to visit me. He mentioned that the staff had never had to prepare for a child being born at the detention center. So, he decided to grant my request and allow my parents to be with me at the hospital for the birth of my child. He said what I did would determine what happened in the future for others in my situation. I thanked God and him. I felt favor from God all around me and I was so thankful that I did not have to be alone at the hospital.

Two nights later, I lost my mucus plug, and my contractions were coming more frequently. Nurse Taylor was on duty that night and she began the process of preparing the staff and me to be escorted to the hospital. I was so excited! I did not know what to expect. The same officer that took me to most of my maternity appointments was called in to transport me to the hospital. I was able to call my parents once I was settled in at the hospital. My mother did not see a reason to come to the hospital until after I delivered my baby. I was so disappointed because I did not have a family member or friend present with me, only the hospital staff and the C.O. It also was perplexing to me that it was standard procedure for inmates to be shackled to the bed. I wondered to myself, "What could I possibly do while I am in labor?" However, there was no reason for me to argue or get upset. Though I knew the Lord was with me, I still felt alone and afraid. The one thing I was excited and happy about was that my baby would finally be free from this atrocious situation. I knew that I would have to return to the detention center without my child, but I was determined to make the best of the moment.

When I asked the detention center staff how long I would have with my child, the answer was it would be my doctor's decision.

My family always said that when a woman is in travail, she has one foot on the Earth and one foot in the grave. I prayed the entire time for God to keep my child and I safe while I was going through this delivery. The head nurse was genuinely nice to me. She took time to explain the entire process. She mentioned that there was a group of nurses selected for me who were trained to support the mother and the child. They would be the only staff that I would see while I was in their care. I was thankful that the hospital staff took the time to plan for my care. They gave me the impression that they cared enough about my child and me to ensure we were safe. Once again, I felt the favor of God all around me. God always amazes me how He is always present — no matter what we are going through. I believed in my heart that this was God's purpose and plan for my child and me because I knew God had the power to change any situation. I had to go through the fire, but God was showing me in so many ways that He was right there with me. Praise Yahweh!

When the nurses prepared me for labor, they fastened a belt on my stomach to hear the baby's heartbeat. My doctor helped my labor along by "breaking my water." My labor pains were increasing as every hour passed and I remained shackled to the bed during this time. I was so nervous, and I had so many thoughts going through my mind. As my labor progressed, I developed pre–eclampsia

(a type of hypertension/high–blood pressure disorder) that creates many pregnancy complications. Specialists say that pre–eclampsia can occur when you are under extremely stressful situations. I had always had normal blood pressure readings at my doctor appointments until now. The attending staff administered medications to help with the labor pains. As time continued passing, the nurses were having a hard time hearing my baby's heartbeat. I started praying to God! My doctor came into my room and said that he was going to prepare me for a C–section birth to minimize the health risk to me and my baby. He said he was not taking a chance because my baby was having complications. As they rolled me into the operating room, the C.O. decided it was time to take the shackles off my legs. The hospital staff continued their kind treatment towards me. I could feel the Spirit of the Lord all around me, keeping me calm, because I was so scared! After I was administered medication to put me in a resting state for the surgery, I was still alert, did not feel any pain, and could see and hear everything that was going on around me. I could see the glory of the Lord in this room resting like a cloud. They had a white sheet placed in front of me, but I was able to see everything in the light fixture above me. I saw them push aside my organs to reach my baby. I saw them pull my child out, cut the umbilical cord, and take the baby to be cleaned up. It was a girl! I was so happy when my baby's pediatric doctor, Dr. Simmons, brought her back in and told me she was the most perfect baby he ever saw, outside of his recently newborn son. He made me laugh and I remember my child's beautiful face. I was able to hold her for a few seconds and then they took her away so that Dr. Washington and the head nurse could finish stitching me up.

Dr. Washington came in to check on me once the nurses had me situated back in my room. He said that the surgery went well, and the stiches were perfect. He said that he expected everything would be fine. I was so thankful to him, the head nurse, and their wonderful staff. Shortly after giving birth to my precious baby girl, I developed an allergic reaction to the anesthesia given to me for surgery. One of the nurses that took care of me came in and offered to rub me down with lotion to help reduce the itching. She was so kind to me; and once again, amid my storm, God was there like Psalm 23:4

(NRSV), "Even though I walk through the darkest valley, I will fear no evil, for You are with me..."

In my mind, this experience was so surreal. With all the negative things that had been said about me in the media, I was thankful to God for the favor that He had placed over my child and me. I do not remember all their names, but they treated me with respect and dignity. I would like to thank every one of them for making my experience a positive memory in such a horrific situation.

After I had time to rest, the nurses brought in my beautiful baby girl.

I remember how that moment of holding my child in my arms made me forget for a few moments that I was once again shackled to the bed and how there were detention officers on "around the clock" duty in my hospital room. I was a new mom with a new baby, and she made my heart melt. She was alive, healthy, beautiful, and perfect! I named her "Halleluyah!" I said that anyone who called her name would have to give praise to my wonderful heavenly Father, Yahweh, El Shaddai!!! One of the nurses immediately got upset with me when she heard me say my child's name. She told me not to give my baby girl this name, but her dissent did not matter. I knew that God alone deserved the glory and giving my baby this name was my way of slapping the devil in the face for all he was trying to do to me and my child. God got the glory and victory — no matter the outcome! I knew my girl was special because Satan had been attacking her while she was in my womb. With all the stress I was under, it was a miracle that I did not have a miscarriage. So, yes, she was given a special name to carry that reverenced God, the great "I Am"! He has a great purpose for her life, and I am tremendously thankful to Him! There is no greater love I have ever experienced than the love from my God!

My baby girl had a good appetite, too. I was so worried that I would not have an opportunity to express enough breast milk, but I was able to feed her from my milk while I was in the hospital. The detention center would not allow me to pump milk for her and have my parents pick it up. This was hurtful but not surprising because I continued to be treated like a criminal rather than a victim of domestic violence. The few people who helped me were a minority because this situation was not handled with any compassion or righteousness. While I was in the hospital, there was an article written about me and my baby. I thought, "Finally, someone had something positive to say about us." This article gave me hope that there were people who believed in my innocence and tried to shine some light on the truth. On the 2nd day after my delivery, I was told that Dr. Washington went out of town. He had left Dr. Tolbert in charge of my care. He was professional and had great bed side manners just like all the other doctors around me. I was surprised that Dr. Washington never said that he was leaving, but I had faith that I was in good care. Dr. Tolbert talked about it being routine for a patient to be hospitalized for (4) days after a C–Section. So, I was determined to maximize the quality time spent with my child. At times, I would cry over her and pray to God about our future. I decided not to dwell on the day that we would be separated, even if just for a moment. I enjoyed watching her. I called my parents to inform them that I had delivered my baby. They arrived with baby items and some maternity items for me. I could see in their eyes that they were worried for me and my child. The C.O. on duty had covered my foot so my parents did not see me shackled to the bed. I was so blessed that my parents were going to take care of my child to avoid her being placed in foster care.

God turned my situation around and gave me favor at the detention center. Everyone could see that I was a person of good character. Many of the staff became friendly with me and used to talk with me about various personal issues. Though friendly, they all remained professional when it came to their jobs.

One of the Staff Sergeants used to bring me chocolate because I had occasional cravings for sweets while I was pregnant. Many female COs had mentioned to me at different times that there was a rumor that one of the fallen officers was my child's father. They also mentioned that everyone was waiting to see who my child would look like. I laughed at this because I could never visualize that as a reality. Besides, I knew that Tyree was my child's father, 100%. I cheated on Tyree once, but that guy was not a cop! So, I ignored the rumor because I knew it was not true. I wondered if this was why Mrs. Tate was so passionate about her speech in court concerning me. I never knew either of the widows' husbands.

When the day finally came for my parents to pick up my child from the hospital, I tried to avoid making eye contact so no one would see the deep hurt in my eyes. I hardly got any sleep. My father followed me in the bathroom, as I packed, to say that he wanted me to cut the locks in my hair. I explained to my father that cutting my hair did not change my skin color, culture, or define my character. With pain in my heart, I told my dad that I was not afraid and was going to trust God. I held Halleluyah in my arms and told her not to forget me.

I told her that I loved her, and that God loved her much more than I ever could.

I tried my best to hold back the tears so that my parents could be strengthened by my courage to peacefully go through this interim guardianship process.

On this day I had two COs escort me back to the detention center.

As my parents were leaving with my baby, the C.O. asked me if I was ready to go. I said "Yes." I took a deep breath with tears rolling down my face as they shackled my hands and feet. I felt a deep ache down in my inner soul that I had never experienced. I prayed to God for the strength to walk every inch of the way. They took me through the back entrance to avoid being seen by the public.

It seemed like a long walk to get to the detention center van. They shackled me inside and locked the van door. The tears started coming profusely and I started shaking and crying hard. This moment hurt so bad! As the van pulled up to the detention center, I asked God to give me the strength to compose myself so I could walk through this place without having an emotional breakdown. I did not want anyone to think that I was weak. As I was escorted into the doors, I suppressed my feelings. When I made it to my bed, I covered my face with the blanket and cried myself to sleep. I felt like I had slept for many hours before I awoke to find my breast sore and fully enlarged with milk. My clothes were soaked too. The nurse on duty helped me to change out of my clothes and put on fresh breast pads.

Lt. Harley came to check on me, as she did at the hospital, to see if I was alright.

I told her that I was still sore, but I was fine. She mentioned to me that my friend Sakina and the other ladies in the women's pod asked about me. Sakina and I became good friends. I asked Lt. Harley to say hello for me and that I was progressively recovering. I said to God that I know my work here was not finished yet or else He would have allowed me to go home and have my baby. Then, I asked God: "What else do you have for me to do here?"

"A wise man will hear and increase learning,
And a man of understanding will attain wise counsel,
To understand a proverb and an enigma,
The words of the wise and their riddles.
The fear of the Lord is the beginning of knowledge,
But fools despise wisdom and instruction."

Proverbs 1:5-7 (NKJV)

"For I consider that the sufferings of this present
time are not worthy to be compared with the
glory which shall be revealed in us.
For the earnest expectation of the creation eagerly
waits for the revealing of the sons of God.
For the creation was subjected to futility, not willingly,
But because of Him who subjected it in hope; because the
creation itself also will be delivered from the bondage of
corruption into the glorious liberty of the children of God.
For we know that the whole creation groans and
labors with birth pangs together until now."

Romans 8:18–22 (NKJV)

CHAPTER 7

❧

OVERCOMING SURVIVOR — BEAT DOWN, CATEGORIZED, AND YET STILL I RISE

STAYED IN THE medical unit until I was released from my doctor, which was (6) weeks later. I was spoiled there because I had my own full bathroom.

The male inmates that worked in the detention center would clean the bathroom every day for me to use the tub. I had fresh towels every day and they would wash my clothes for me. I praised God for His continued favor! I knew I was going to miss this treatment when I went back to the women's pod, but I missed my friend Sakina. She was my workout buddy and my baby's godmother. The C.O.s would tease us and said we were twins joined at the hip! I could not wait to rejoin her to resume working out. I did not hear from my attorneys since delivering my baby. I was wondering when the court date for my 3rd bond hearing was going to be.

I was told by an older inmate that murder trials usually take more than a year to go to trial. She said there was much preparation involved. I had no clue about what was going to happen, but I was hopeful. I told God that if it was meant for me to go to prison, then just be with me.

My dad came often to visit me. He made sure I had money in my canteen account. He would encourage me to "hang in there" and told me that he believed in my innocence. He said he believed that I was coming home to my baby too.

He would bring Halleluyah to see me when he could. Those visits were hard! I was not allowed to have any contact visits with her. I could only see her through a glass window. My mom would come sometimes with my father, but she would come with a negative attitude. I understood that this situation was hard. I imagined that life was complicated for my parents, especially when many people are hating you & your child but do not know the truth. I continued to pray for my family that God would protect them from anyone trying to harm them.

Months passed before I heard anything definite about my case. I received a letter from my attorney, Mr. Hart that stated that my 3rd bond hearing was scheduled. I occupied my time the best I could by working out with Sakina and studying my Bible. One thing was for sure, I gained a closer, more intimate relationship with the Lord. I continued to pray (3) times a day and Sakina &

I would fast together. My hair had gotten so much longer, too. I had been incarcerated in the county lock up for almost 8.5 months before I had my 3rd bond hearing.

I had a visitor that told me I was a target of discrimination. His name was Israel. He brought me two newspaper articles — one written about a Caucasian female that was on the scene when her boyfriend shot and killed a police officer, and the other one about an Asian female that was accused of killing her rich Caucasian husband on Hilton Head. The familiarity to my case slapped me in the face. He informed me that if someone had the money to bail me out, they could not! Mr. Israel was right. I thought about this and how illegal this entire situation was. So many of my constitutional rights had been violated. I was not a threat to society, no flight risk, nor had I ever committed any violent crimes. Yet, I still could not get bailed out on bond.

My child was almost (4) months old and I remember that it became so much harder to look at my child from a window. I longed to hold her again. I finally told my parents not to bring my child back for visits because it hurt too much. I would cry for hours after the visits and I told God that I could not take it any longer, and something had to change. There was no guarantee that this bond hearing was going to result in freedom, but my dream gave me hope. My father had said to me on one of his visits that he believed that God was going to set me free this time.

He said that God had shown him in a dream that it was time. Sakina joined me in fasting for the entire week leading up to my bond hearing. I re–twisted my hair in preparation for my court appearance because I was sure the media would be there taking pictures.

My attorneys paid me a visit before I was due in court. They talked to me about their expectations of how the bond hearing would proceed. They were also hopeful. When the C.O. came to escort me to court, I remember feeling boldly confident than any other time of going to court. I made up in my mind that I was going to trust God and block out any thoughts of doubt. As I walked into the courtroom, I looked up to camera flashes in my face. I sat down in the middle of my attorneys and looked around to see my supporting family and friends.

The judge heard both sides of the arguments for why I should and should not receive a bail bond. Judge Mathews resided again, and he asked the state if they had a court date set for me. The state replied "No". He said he was going to set a bond. I got so excited about what I was hearing! Now, we waited to see how much the bond would be. The judge set my bond at $40,000 and he told the state that they needed to set a court date. The solicitor asked the judge to send me home with an ankle monitor, but Judge Mathews denied his request. I could have done cartwheels on my walk back to the detention center. I was so happy!!! The most important thing that happened to me was that God blessed me to go home to my baby girl, Halleluyah. Praise GOD!!!

"Now to Him who is able to do exceedingly
abundantly above all that we ask or think,
according to the power that works in us,
To Him be glory in the church by Christ Jesus to
all generations, forever and ever. Amen."
Ephesians 3:20–21 (NKJV)

My first and ultimate thanks goes to GOD Almighty.
This story, in its fullness, has been inspired by the Holy Spirit.
By finishing this book, I have realized how blessed
I was to experience how marvelous my loving GOD is,
especially while I was going through such a tormented storm.
There were multiple times I could have been killed,
but GOD protected me.
There were multiple times that I should have lost my mind,
but GOD blocked the adversary from destroying me.
I am a living testimony
that even in the midst of many storms of life,
when the situation looks like it will take you out,
you can make it!
GOD will never leave you nor will He ever forsake you!

FINAL NOTE

*This book debut is just the beginning
of "In The Life of Nzuri."
If you enjoyed reading this segment,
stay tuned for the sequel.*

*If you or anyone you know is a victim (or
suspected victim) of any type of abuse
or in need of family & youth services,
be encouraged to reach out to the following 24/7 lifeline —
accessible in 170 languages
and available in the U.S, Puerto Rico,
Guam, and the U.S. Virgin Islands:*

National Domestic Violence Hotline
(Family & Youth Services Bureau)
@
800.799. SAFE (7233)
800.787.3224 (TTY)
206.518.9361 (Deaf Callers Only)
or
https://www.acf.hhs.gov/fysb/programs

Printed in the United States
By Bookmasters